THE DANCE OF LIGHT NOVELLA

THE KNIGHT OF THE MOON

Gregory Kontaxis

GK

To everyone who believed in me

Contents

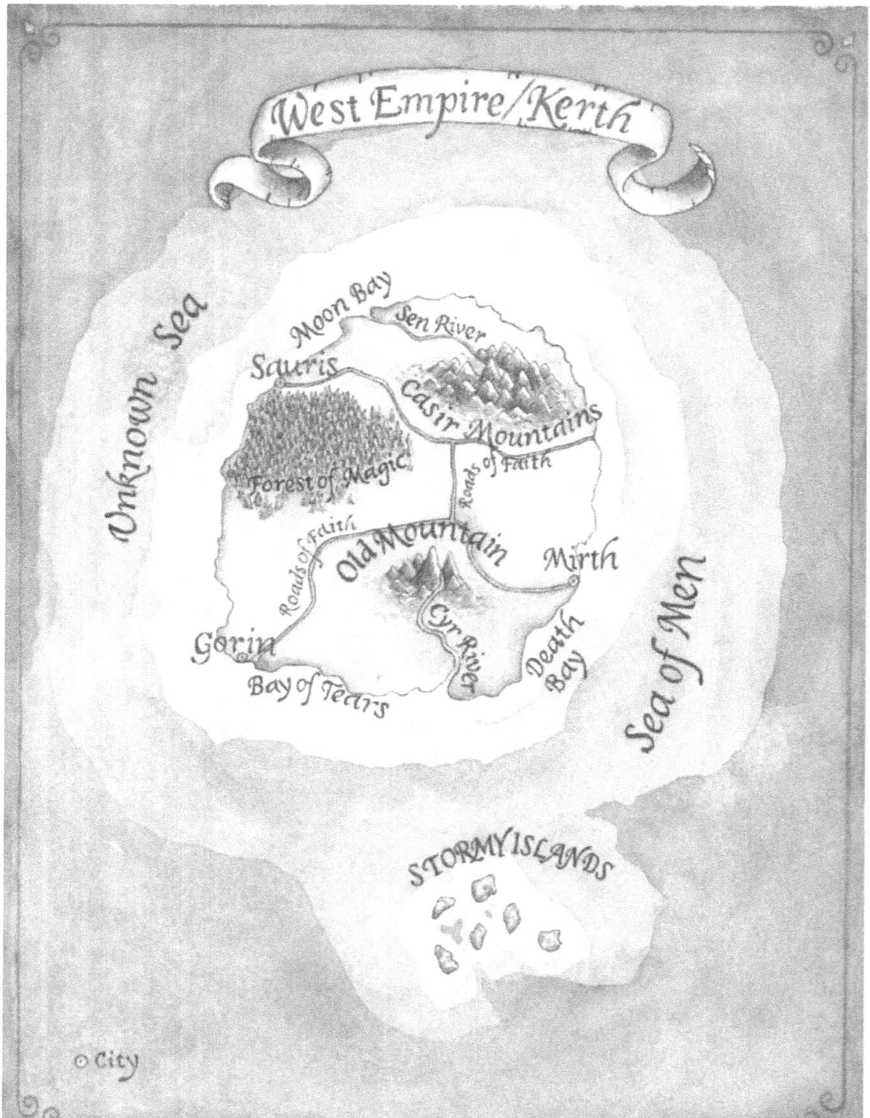

West Empire/Kerth
Unknown Sea
Moon Bay
Sen River
Sauris
Casir Mountains
Roads of Faith
Forest of Magic
Roads of Faith
Old Mountain
Mirth
Gorin
Cyr River
Death Bay
Sea of Men
Bay of Tears
STORMY ISLANDS
City

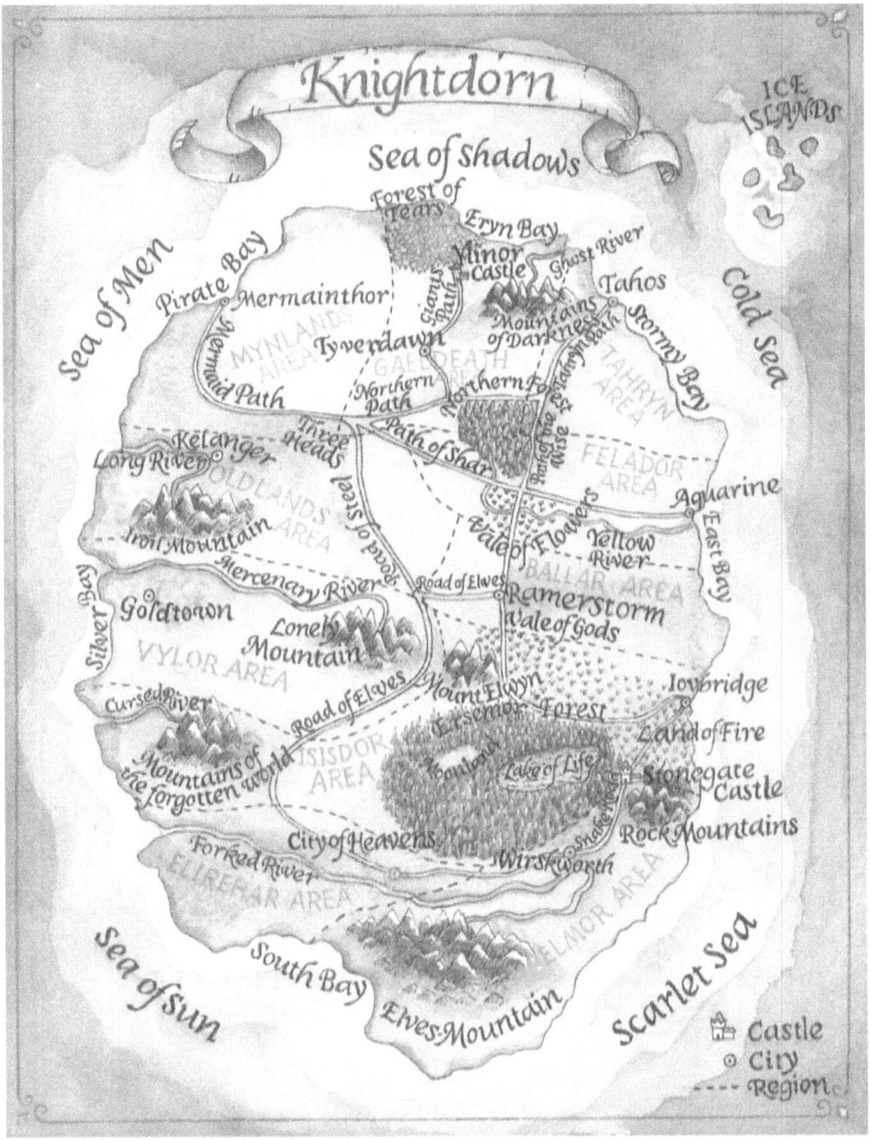

Knightdorn

ICE ISLANDS

Sea of Shadows

Sea of Men

Cold Sea

Forest of Tears

Eryn Bay

Minor Castle

Ghost River

Tahos

Pirate Bay

Mermainthor

MYNLANDS AREA

Mermaid Path

Tyverdawn

Giant's Path

GAELDEATH

Mountains of Darkness

Stormy Bay

TAHRYN AREA

Path of the Pendragon

Northern Path

Northern Forest

FELADOR AREA

Three Heads

Path of Shar

Kelanger

Long River

OLDLANDS AREA

Road of Steel

Aguarine

East Bay

Iron Mountain

Vale of Flowers

Yellow River

Mercenary River

Road of Elves

BALLAR AREA

Silver Bay

Goldtonn

Lonely Mountain

VYLOR AREA

Ramerstorm

Vale of Gods

Cursed River

Road of Elves

Mount Elwyn

Iovbridge

Ersemor Forest

Land of Fire

Mountains of the forgotten world

ISISDOR AREA

Fhoulown

Lake of Life

Stonegate Castle

City of Heavens

Snakehead

Wirskworth

Rock Mountains

Forked River

ELIREHAR AREA

ELMIOR AREA

Sea of Sun

South Bay

Elves Mountain

Scarlet Sea

Castle

City

Region

The Phoenix

John lifted his cup to his mouth and swigged a mouthful of wine. The woman opposite him was smiling. He tried, unsuccessfully, to stay focused on her face while his eyes kept wandering down to her breasts that spilled out from her woollen dress, and his mind pictured what he hoped would later follow.

"Are you a regular here?" the woman asked him.

"Yeah, The Phoenix is one of the best places in town," said John, choking down a burp.

The woman sipped her wine, her gaze sultry.

"I haven't seen you here before, love," John muttered softly. His eyes momentarily swept across the inside of the inn. A couple dozen men sitting on wooden benches were drinking themselves into a stupor while a handful of women glanced around anxiously, waiting for someone to approach them. Soon, night would fall, and John knew that The Phoenix would fill with patrons, as well as prostitutes.

"It's my first time here. My sister told me this is the best place to find..." The woman's voice trailed off in the middle of her sentence and she shifted in her chair, avoiding his gaze.

"That's a fact," John replied smiling, putting her out of the difficult situation. "I'd be willing to bet you recently decided to... keep men company for gold."

"Why would you say that, my lord?"

"I'm no lord." John smacked his lips, taking another gulp of wine. "Every woman who does this kind of work knows that The Phoenix is the inn with the most clientele. You said this is your first time here…"

The woman's gaze was pinned on him; her eyes were honey-coloured, with golden speckles. She had plush, full lips, generous breasts, and a playful smile that could capture the heart of anyone. John was lucky that he'd sought to talk to her before every other sleaze at The Phoenix that night.

"Why did you decide to become…" he lowered his voice, "a whore?"

"Does it matter?"

"I'm just curious."

The woman frowned. "I worked my father's fields for next to nothing. My sister gave up a while ago. She became a prostitute and, gathered enough gold within a few days to buy a mare and travel to Kelanger. There, she married a local lord, and now they have two sons. Had I stayed in the fields, I would have never left that place."

"Your village is near Three Heads?"

The woman nodded yes.

"What is your name?"

"Myla."

John's eyes wandered down once more to the breasts ready to escape from her dress. "I'm sure a woman with your beauty will quickly make her way out of here. Merchants and nobles come to Three Heads from miles around. I'd bet that before long, someone will sweep you off your feet and steal you away once and for all."

"Perhaps that someone could be you, my lord," she said in a sensual tone.

"I've told you, I'm no lord." John knew she hadn't believed him. Most nobles tended to conceal their titles when looking for prostitutes at Three Heads, the famous crossroad of the north. John had even heard that governors came to this place in disguise, in order to spend a few nights with beautiful women without the news reaching their spouses. Consequently, every prostitute's dream was that a lord would fall in love with her and leave his wife.

"Your clothes look like they're made from the finest silk," Myla said.

John's right hand stroked his blue jerkin. "I'm just good at my job."

Myla's teeth caught on her lip. "Then, would you want a wife with beauty like mine?"

John felt desire sparking within his core. The woman facing him had the most innocent, yet seductive face he'd ever seen. If that wasn't enough, he liked that she wasn't too young, like some of the girls who sold themselves before their breasts had even budded.

"I'm not the kind of man you'd want for a husband, love," he told her.

"Why not?" Myla teased playfully.

"I travel the whole kingdom to earn my gold. You don't want a man who'll never be home."

Myla supped a few gulps of the crimson wine in her cup and licked her lips. "Perhaps, after tonight, you'll change your mind. What's your name?"

"John."

"What do you say we go to your room, John?"

John downed the contents of his cup. "I thought Fate was already kind to me, sending me good fortune. Still, I never dared to think I'd have the luck to spend the night with a woman like you, Myla."

In one swift movement, John got up, and Myla followed. He moved to her side and slid his arm around her waist while she softly leaned towards his face.

"I promise that you'll never forget tonight," she whispered, leaning forward to nibble his ear.

Heat flooded his whole body. He wanted to bend her over the wooden counter and take her right there, ignoring the rest of the inn.

A sudden slamming of a door forced him to turn his head. A dozen armed soldiers wearing red cloaks had stormed into the inn. John momentarily forgot about Myla and studied their faces. *Soldiers of Gaeldeath.*

"Which of you is John the Long Arm?" yelled one of the newcomers.

Panic surged through John's chest. The soldiers of Gaeldeath often hunted men down to bring them to justice or kill them. He searched for an escape. The best possible option was to conceal every trace of surprise and head to his room upstairs. Myla seemed frightened by the presence of the newcomers.

"I heard that the Long Arm came to this inn. Where is he?" the soldier demanded once more.

Nobody spoke up.

Drawing his sword, the soldier headed towards a counter in the centre of the inn. Behind it stood an elderly, bewildered man.

"If you don't tell me where John is, I'll make you choke on your shrivelled cullions," the soldier spat.

The old man's face went red. Time seemed to flow like molasses, and John's legs stiffened as the wrinkled hand of the elder slowly pointed towards him.

The Outlaw Knight

Night had fallen, and John felt his end was drawing near. He marched, surrounded by the soldiers that had escorted him out of The Phoenix a few moments earlier. He was lucky they didn't cuff him. His heart hammered against his ribcage. *They want to kill me away from prying eyes.* He repeated this thought again and again, but it didn't quite make sense; the soldiers of Gaeldeath wouldn't hesitate to kill in plain sight. *Perhaps they want to take me to Tyverdawn.*

Cold sweat ran down his forehead, yet his eyes kept finding the young woman wearing shiny armour and a red cloak. Her demeanour was cold while her chestnut hair bounced on her shoulders. John didn't recognize her and the sight of her among the other soldiers made her stand out. Northerners didn't tend to have female warriors.

As the soldiers took him further from The Phoenix, John noticed one more inn on their way to wherever they were taking him. The Green Gate had the most palatable wine in Three Heads. If he was going to die, he would have liked to have had one last decent drink.

The men leading the way halted, and John came to a sudden stop, feeling his hands go numb and his mouth dry up.

"What do you want from me?" he demanded, clumsily hiding his dread.

"I've heard plenty of stories about you, Long Arm. I'd expect a known bounty hunter such as yourself to have a little more pluck," said the man who had shouted for him earlier at The Phoenix. He was a tall, well-built soldier with a bushy beard.

"You don't need pluck to become a bounty hunter..." John told him.

"What d'you need, then?"

"Brains. Most men of war are brave and lethal with a sword but lack common sense."

The man watched him for a couple of moments before breaking into hearty laughter. The rest of the soldiers joined in while the woman regarded him silently with black eyes. "Who are you?" John asked the man.

"My name's Yorik, and I'm Gaeldeath's captain."

"And what do you want from me?"

The captain scratched his chin, while his tiny, sunken eyes watched John thoughtfully. "I need you to take care of some business for me."

John had thought of every possible reason as to why the soldiers might need to talk to him—except this one. "What kind of business?" he asked.

"To find someone and bring me their head as soon as possible," said Yorik.

"One would think that Robert Thorn had thousands of soldiers for this purpose. Why would you need me?"

The soldiers started laughing again, and John looked at them with confusion.

"Robert Thorn isn't the Governor of Gaeldeath anymore," Yorik responded.

John swore his eyes couldn't get any wider. "Robert Thorn is dead?"

"No. His son rebelled against him and assumed his office. The lords and the council backed him, and like that, Robert and his wife were exiled from Gaeldeath. According to the information given to us, they ran to the king's side on horseback."

"Walter exiled his own father?" Yorik nodded, and John frowned. "Even so, I don't understand why Walter needs my help."

"Walter has many plans to execute and needs every soldier he can get. I asked around, and the general opinion seems to be that you're the best bounty hunter in the north. If you bring me the head of the man I'm seeking, you'll be rewarded with a great deal of gold."

John scratched his chin. What he was hearing was both intriguing and daunting. It was certain that the Gaeldean Soldiers would pay good money for this bounty, but he would bet that the man they were looking for was dangerous.

"Who is the man you're seeking, then?"

"Gareth Huneywood."

John nearly choked. "The Knight of the Moon?"

Yorik nodded, his expression unchanging.

"Typically, my services are needed by merchants and small-time nobles who want to collect their gold from cheating debtors. I'm not the right man to kill a knight."

"I've heard that John the Long Arm has never failed in completing a bounty."

"But—"

"Listen to me!" Yorik cut in. "This mission was entrusted to my highers-up by Walter himself. I refuse to waste men, and I refuse to fail! If in ten days you haven't returned to Three Heads with the knight's head, you'll gain a bounty on your own head worth ten thousand gold pieces. Everyone will be after you; there will be no place to hide."

John felt everything shrink around him. "I've never faced a knight in my life! On top of that, I haven't the faintest idea where Gareth could be. Ten days isn't enough!"

Yorik smiled. "I have some information that might help you... That lech was smitten with a lady from the House of Arden—Alis. However, due to his knight's oaths, he couldn't marry her even though he wanted to. Alis' parents wanted to marry her off to another lord, and she snuck herself out of the city, refusing to wed anyone but Gareth."

"You think that Gareth is with her?"

Yorik nodded in agreement. "I've heard rumours that Alis has fled to the Iron Mountain, but they are not proven. Still, perhaps this knowledge might be useful in finding Gareth before I put a bounty on your head."

John sized Yorik up. He looked like the type of man who followed through with his threats.

"Gareth ran away to live with Alis, and that's why Walter wants to punish him?"

Yorik's brow furrowed. "Not just for that. That cur didn't approve of Walter's nomination for governor, and when he left Tyverdawn, he left a letter... A letter that declared he'd only recognise Robert as the true Governor of Gaeldeath. Traitor!" Yorik spat on the ground.

"The King's decrees state that no governor can be replaced before his death. I'd bet that Walter will soon have to face the Royal Army for his own betrayal," said John.

"Don't you dare call Walter a traitor again!" Yorik yelled, now red-faced. The rest of the soldiers seemed irritated too. "The only one who betrayed the north is his father. The Royal Army isn't your problem—just make sure to bring me Gareth's head in ten days."

"How do you know the knight isn't by Robert's side? If he set out to find his old governor, it'd be impossible to catch him in the royal capital."

"Our informants are monitoring every road that leads to Iovbridge, and nobody has seen Gareth. If you find evidence that he's under the king's wing, show it to me, and I will let you keep your head."

John didn't want this mission, but he was in favour of staying alive. "Alright," he said after a few moments.

He was ready to turn around and leave when he heard Yorik's voice again.

"Nemesis will accompany you on this mission."

John saw him looking at the dark-eyed woman with the shining armour.

"No!" he snapped. "I don't need help. If I fail, put a bounty on me!" insisted John, looking at Yorik. He never wanted people he didn't trust on his missions.

"You're not in a position to negotiate, Long Arm. She won't come with you solely to help, but to atone for her actions. She could recognise Gareth, so she might be useful—if you fail, she will face the same fate as you."

With these words, Yorik gave a dismissive jerk of his head and started heading off with the rest of the soldiers.

John remained frozen where he was before turning his head towards Nemesis. Her eyes were boring into him, her icy gaze impenetrable.

The Blind Rat

John cast a last look at Nemesis and huffed with indignation. "Curse your name, Walter Thorn!" he hissed then started to walk off hurriedly.

"Where are you going?" the woman asked.

"To save my life, and yours too," John replied. Out of the corner of his eye, he saw Nemesis following him, matching his swift pace. The woman had fierce eyes yet her features were youthful and beautiful.

"What are you planning to do?"

"I don't report to you!" John snapped at her angrily.

"We're on this mission together. We have to agree on a plan," she ordered.

John swivelled around to face her. "We don't need to agree on anything! I can't trust you. I'll find a way to kill that knight. You can do the same, and maybe one of us will succeed."

He turned to leave once more when he felt cold steel against his neck.

"The mission Yorik gave you is hard, and should we fail, we will die. We're going to lay out a plan together, and you will inform me before you make a move," Nemesis told him.

Turning around, John's body shook with rage. He had to find a way to succeed in this mission, while a stranger gave him orders. "You think you're in a position to dictate to me? You need me! You can't possibly hope to find the Knight of the Moon without me..."

"You're sure I need you?" Nemesis pressed the blade to his throat.

John froze, the steel cold against his skin. "Do you really know how to use a sword, or was it a toy that your rich daddy bought you?"

Nemesis brought her face close to his, her eyes narrowed. "Don't you dare belittle me again, or I'll cut your hands off."

Something in her eyes told him that she planned to follow through with her promise.

"Very well..." muttered John. If nothing else, she'd earned his respect.

"What are you planning?" Nemesis demanded.

"I'll meet with a man I know," *That was the only way... He had to ask guidance from the old man.*

The sword didn't leave his throat, making it clear that it would stay there until he offered more detail.

"The Blind Rat knows everything that goes on in Knightdorn," said John.

"The Blind Rat?" she repeated, arching an eyebrow.

"It's a nickname. Nobody knows his actual name," John elaborated.

"That much I could guess. And why would he be giving you information?"

"He's always been fond of my sense of humour..."

Nemesis' glare almost burned through him.

"That and I caught a couple cheats who owed him money, while often taking him out for drinks and... well, whores," added John staring at the moon in the night sky.

Nemesis' sword was lowered a couple of centimetres. "I don't expect such a good informant to come from a place like Three Heads."

"You'd be surprised... We are at the crossroad of the north. Many find what they seek here. Although, if you'd been a bounty hunter, you'd know the most important lesson of the trade."

"That being?"

"Many times, the hardest thing isn't finding someone but catching them."

In one fluid motion, Nemesis returned her sword to its sheath. John could tell by the way she sheathed her sword that she was a well-trained warrior—he shouldn't have underestimated her. He wondered why Gaeldeath's soldiers had forced him to take her with him. *What had she done that she needed to atone for?*

"Follow me," John said.

He started walking along the flat road, and the woman followed close by. They passed The Phoenix and moved along the road that cut through Three Heads. John scanned the taverns around them, searching for a specific one. After a little while, he noticed a smoking chimney, and saw men eating and drinking through the sparse, square windows. Recognising The Dripping Bucket by a dirty brown flag, he started walking towards the building's small entrance.

He pushed the wooden door open with force and stepped inside, with Nemesis behind him. He glanced at the woman's breastplate—he didn't want to draw attention to the fact that he was bringing a soldier into the inn.

"This is where we'll find the man you're looking for?" Nemesis asked.

"That's right... He was always fond of The Dripping Bucket."

Nemesis studied their surroundings with a critical eye, nostrils flaring with disdain. "I wonder why. This is the filthiest place I've ever seen."

"The Dripping Bucket is full of men that like to remain inconspicuous..."

"And why would an informant be here?"

"In this kind of place, you can gather a lot of information," John replied cryptically.

He slowly paced along the wooden corridor between the tables and looked around. Dozens of men sat about, speaking in whispers. The Dripping Bucket wasn't for drunken young men and obnoxiously loud wenches. A few more steps later, he saw an elderly man with long, silvery white hair and a thick beard. John and Nemesis approached him, and the man turned his gaze towards them.

"I know that smell," the man said. "It's been a while, Long Arm."

John looked into his empty eye-sockets. He had always wondered how the man could notice his presence without being able to see him. Now he knew.

The old man turned to Nemesis this time. "I don't remember having been approached before by this woman," he noted.

John cast a look towards Nemesis who was examining the stranger curiously.

"We need to talk," John said dryly.

"Something troubles you, Long Arm. I can hear it in your voice. I've got a few more things to discuss with my friend, but perhaps that can wait." The old man nodded, and the man opposite him got up and left silently.

The Blind Rat made a little gesture with his hand, as if asking them to sit. John and Nemesis took the bench across from him.

"I need some information," said John.

"Is this somehow related to Gaeldeath's soldiers dragging you out of The Phoenix earlier today?"

John felt frustration mixed with curiosity. This blind man seemed to know everything. "Yes."

"I don't know what you're looking for, but if I can help you, I will. However, it's best that we talk in private. You know I don't like speaking to strangers." His sightless eyes seemed to shift to Nemesis.

"Nemesis is a friend," John said.

"Nemesis? Never heard of a name like that before, but I like it. Still, I don't want to speak in front of her."

"You don't have a choice," Nemesis cut in.

John turned towards Nemesis, signalling her to hush. She shot back an angry glare.

"Is that right?" the elderly man asked. "If I refuse to speak in front of you, will you unsheathe the sword on your belt and kill me?"

Nemesis didn't reply.

The Blind Rat rubbed his grizzled chin. "Very well. I'll accept you staying with us under one condition."

"What condition?" the woman asked.

"When I tell you all I know, if there is anything relevant to what you're looking for, I will ask you something and you must answer it, whatever it may be."

Nemesis sized him up. "Fine."

"What information are you looking for, Long Arm?" the Blind Rat asked, smiling.

John looked at the greasy, white hair hanging on the old man's shrivelled form. "Gaeldeath's men told me that Walter Thorn—"

"Exiled his father. I know that Walter is the new Governor of Gaeldeath."

John was no longer surprised by the man's knowledge. "A knight deserted the moment Robert was exiled, and Walter wants his head."

"The Knight of the Moon. Yes. He is the only knight of Gaeldeath who still lives."

"What do you mean?" asked John.

The Blind Rat laughed. "The other knights are dead. Perhaps the lords and the council could betray Robert, but at least his knights remained loyal to him. Walter killed them just before he sent his father away. Gareth managed to get away. I heard that Robert told him to leave the city when he realised Walter would take power."

John rested his elbows on the table, leaning forward.

"I suppose you want help finding the Knight of the Moon. Those soldiers assigned you this mission?"

John huffed with exhaustion. "Yes... Walter didn't want to waste men on that."

"Naturally... His mother is the king's sister. Thomas Egercoll will try to punish him for what he did to Robert. However, Walter can't face the king with just Gaeldeath's army..." The Blind Rat lowered his voice.

John mulled over his words. "I bet Walter will try to unite the north against Thomas, and should he fail, he'll probably try to subjugate the northern regions. He'll need every man he can get for something like that."

"I agree," the old man said.

"But if all of this is true, why would Walter bother himself with a knight? One would think there'd be more important matters that merit his attention."

"I'm certain you don't know Walter. In his eyes, a man that betrayed his knight's oaths deserves punishment."

"He exiled his own father!" John exclaimed.

"Walter believes his father betrayed Gaeldeath when he joined their house with the king's," Nemesis threw back.

"Precisely," the old man hummed approvingly.

"Enough of all this," John cut in. "I've got ten days to find Gareth, otherwise I'll lose my head. The soldiers told me that he was in love with some lady, and they could be together. However, I'm worried that the knight might be by Robert's side, making it impossible to get my hands on him."

The old man shook his head. "Gareth is with Alis in a village near the Iron Mountain. I don't know where exactly, but if you ride up as far as the Long River by the mountain fringes, I think you'll manage to find them. The villagers might help you if you offer some gold."

"And you're sure Gareth is there?

"You know that I like you too much to wish your demise, Long Arm," replied the blind man with a smile while the soft glow of the candles made his hollow eye sockets gleam. "I hope you manage to find him."

John thought for a few moments. *I have to leave for the Iron Mountain with the first light.* Then, he moved to stand.

"One moment," the old man said. "Nemesis needs to pay the price for all she heard."

"What's the question?" the woman asked with a steady voice.

"When you walked by my table and sat by Long Arm's side, I could tell from the sound you made that you're in armour. John and his friends don't tend to wear plate armour... I suppose that you're a soldier—a soldier of Gaeldeath. I'd bet that the other troops ordered you to join John on this mission, although I can't tell why. They wanted to humiliate you? They weren't fond of the fact that a woman bore the title of soldier?"

"Those men didn't order me to do anything," Nemesis replied, her cold expression revealing nothing.

"Interesting... Then, perhaps Walter wanted to punish you for something you did. I'm guessing that helping to find the Knight of the Moon is a way to redeem yourself," said the Blind Rat.

"Yes. If I wasn't well-liked, Walter would have killed me instead of giving me this... *opportunity*." Her voice betrayed her bewilderment at how the Blind Rat could deduce this much.

"What did you do?" the old man whispered.

"All of this is starting to sound like more than one question," Nemesis replied.

"But I'm sure you want to tell us. I could feel the rage in your voice the whole time you spoke. Besides, if you are to accompany Long Arm on this mission, it's best he knows who you really are."

John looked at Nemesis questioningly. The woman's eyes sparked.

"What did you do?" the old man repeated.

"A soldier, the son of a lord that Walter held in high regard, tried to rape me a few days ago."

"And?" the Blind Rat probed.

"I killed him," she said through clenched teeth.

Now, even John could feel the rage in Nemesis' tone.

"How?" the old man whispered.

Nemesis leaned towards him, eyes glowing like hot coals under the dim candlelight. "I chopped off his cock and stuffed it in his mouth while he bled out."

With those words, Nemesis stood and made for the exit of the tavern. John stared at her back as she left, stunned, until he heard the Blind Rat's voice.

"I like that woman."

The Knight's Tale

Nemesis pulled on the reins of the black horse she'd recently bought as she walked alongside it. The forest around her became thicker and thicker while the beast resisted her pull, slowing her down.

"Damn it," she hissed and continued pulling the horse along. Long Arm had told her she'd be needing a reliable steed for their journey.

She hadn't been able to sleep in the inn's stony bed the previous night, rage licking at her insides like hellfire and leaving her without a moment's peace. She never expected to be setting off on a mission with an unknown bounty hunter. A mission that was her only hope of returning home. She thought about how rage had flooded her soul all these years; she remembered the self-assured boys that mocked her, back when she first sought to learn how to fight, and her father who shouted at her that if she wanted to make anything of herself in life, her best chance was by seducing a rich lord.

Nemesis loved her parents, even if they were short-sighted. They never listened to anything she told them. She wasn't made for marriage and childrearing. Inside her burned a warrior's flame.

She recalled the first knights' jousting tournament she'd watched in Gaeldeath. The knights of Mynlands and of Tahryn had travelled to the regional capital, giving her the chance to see great warriors battling. She could still remember the military drills in the city's courtyards, the soldiers bearing swords and bows. She had tried countless times to hold a sword, to learn to grip it correctly. However, the young men always treated her with disdain, laughing and jeering. Every time, she'd throw down the sword at her feet and leave, cursing her lack of skill.

Rage had been boiling restlessly inside Nemesis' soul as far back as she could remember, until one day, she couldn't take it anymore. She had grabbed a bow and arrow from the ground while watching some children learning archery and taken aim. Her arrow buried itself in the very centre of the target, and the angry stares of the boys, who had failed in their attempts, filled her with even more rage.

"Don't you dare come to our training again!" one of the boys had shouted.

"I'd say you should want this young woman training with you. I'm sure there's much to learn from her," a voice had said.

Erneas, the Grand Master of Gaeldeath, had witnessed her feat and was looking at her with great interest.

"What is your name, dear?" he'd asked.

"Nemesis."

Erneas had appreciated her talent, and with time, had come to love her as a daughter. The Grand Master had sought to talk to her parents about her gift in battle.

"If she's such a gifted warrior, why don't you train her?" her father had asked.

"I'm the Grand Master of Gaeldeath. My responsibility is to train the future knights of the region. Even if I regret the fact that knights are exclusively men by law, I cannot change it."

"King Thomas allowed women to rise to the title of governor and queen, and he won't allow them to take a knight's oaths?"

Erneas had frowned. *"Thomas believes that women are fit to lead, but not to fight. Perhaps with time, he'll reconsider."*

Nemesis adored Erneas. Even if he couldn't train her himself, he'd insisted that she was taught the art of battle by the drillmasters of the region. As time went by, she managed to earn the respect of hundreds of Gaeldeath's soldiers while also enrolling into Tyverdawn's guard. In this way, her rage had been soothed—until everything went wrong. A drunken lecher had tried to rape her, and her actions had pitted her against Walter Thorn. She knew that the new governor's father wouldn't send her on a mission like this. Robert Thorn punished rapists severely, no matter what noble house's name they bore. She was lucky that Erneas had taken her side, along with a considerable number of captains and commanders. Something inside her told her that Walter wouldn't show her mercy under different circumstances. There were many in Gaeldeath who were still loyal to his father, and he didn't want to create discord. Still, Lord Astor, the father of the man she'd killed, was Walter's ally, and so Nemesis had to at least be punished.

She continued dragging her horse between the trees, looking for Long Arm. He'd found her outside The Dripping Bucket the previous night and asked her to meet him at dawn in a small forest west of Three Heads. Nemesis had spent the night in an inn, away from the drunk men and whores that were common in the area. She wanted to think; she knew that this was practically a suicide mission. It'd be an impossible feat to find the Knight of the Moon and deliver his head to Walter within ten days. They didn't have an army, and even Gaeldeath's informants had failed to find any clues as to Sir Gareth's whereabouts. She felt rage burning inside her once more. She had to find forgiveness for killing the man who had tried to rape her.

She kept walking, and John came to her mind. She never liked bounty hunters; they had neither honour nor loyalty to anyone. She recalled John talking to a whore as she and the rest of Gaeldeath's soldiers had approached him. Men like him would sell their kids for wine and prostitutes. However, there was something strange about John. She had seen respect in his eyes when she had raised her sword and ordered him to obey her. Then, the moment she revealed what she had done to the man who tried to rape her, she swore that John had looked at her with admiration. Bounty hunters didn't respect women, but John seemed different in this respect. A part of her wanted to learn more about him. He seemed different and that made him interesting.

Her horse neighed loudly and shook its large body, trying to escape her hands. Nemesis yanked on the reins and brought her face near to the horse's.

"Like it or not, we're going to stick together for the coming days," she whispered, softly stroking its head. The beast snorted before calming under her touch.

Nemesis ran her fingers through the horse's mane, and resumed walking, slowly. This time, the beast followed her without an issue. As they continued along, the trees became denser the deeper as they delved into the forest. Warmth enveloped her body under her leather clothes and steel breastplate. This day was warmer than its predecessors; winter would soon give way to spring.

"Finally! I thought you'd never come."

Nemesis turned and saw Long Arm dressed in brown wool garments, standing next to two other men. One was of average height and build, with a bow and a quiver full of arrows slung over his shoulder; the other was huge and had a long sword hanging on his belt. Three horses waited next to them.

"I was under the impression we'd travel alone," Nemesis snapped, looking at the unknown men suspiciously.

"Alan and Edric are my partners in every mission I undertake. I've briefed them on everything that's happened," said John.

"I thought you worked alone," Nemesis continued, taking a brief look at the short sword tied to Long Arm's belt.

"If I did work alone, I wouldn't be the most famous bounty hunter in the kingdom. Alan is one of the best archers I've ever met. Edric is helpful when things go wrong. I think it's obvious why," Long Arm grinned, looking at Edric's giant form.

Nemesis took a closer look at John's companions. The archer, Alan, wore leather trousers and a green vest, while the taller man, Edric, was dressed in dark red fabric. His brutish face—it was too small for his body and looked like his head was glued onto his shoulders—gave her the impression he was not the sharpest arrow in the quiver.

Alan took a step towards her. "John told us that Gaeldeath's soldiers ordered you to follow us on this journey. John has his wits while I have my bow, and Edric, his brawn. What do you have to offer?" he asked with a mocking tone.

Nemesis felt her fingers itch with the urge to unsheathe her blade. "I've got my sword, and if I detect a note of sarcasm in your voice again, I won't hesitate to use it."

"I hope you're a warrior in practice, and not just in theory," Alan continued.

"Perhaps if you knew the reason I'm here, you'd watch your mouth."

Alan smiled. "Oh, I know. Although, the poor son of a lord is hardly a worthy opponent."

Nemesis was ready to reply, enraged, when Alan drew the bow from his shoulder in a flash. Nemesis let go of her horse's reins and twisted her body to the side, avoiding the arrow. Immediately, her sword was unsheathed and her body straightened. *You're dead.*

Before she could sprint towards Alan, he'd returned his bow to his shoulder.

"No need to attack me," Alan told her.

Nemesis looked at him from behind her brandished steel. "You attacked first."

"I wanted to find out the truth. You truly are a warrior."

Nemesis lowered her sword a fraction. The sarcasm had left his voice. John smiled, while Edric seemed completely indifferent to his surroundings.

"We should be going," Long Arm reminded them. "I'd advise you to leave your cloak behind."

Nemesis sheathed her sword. "Why?"

"We're looking for a knight of your region. If we travel with cloaks bearing Gaeldeath's emblem, we'll be more conspicuous than we'd like."

He's right. Nemesis should have thought of that.

"The armour would draw suspicion, too," Alan chimed in.

"There's no way I'm leaving my breastplate in a forest." Nemesis could never throw away a gift from Erneas.

"Very well," said John, mounting his horse.

Nemesis took off her red cloak adorned with its white tiger, and left it by the trunk of a tree. She returned to her horse, which thankfully hadn't run away the moment she'd let go of its reins, and climbed into the saddle.

"Where did you get that horse?" Alan asked.

"From a merchant near The Phoenix."

"Handsome beast. I haven't seen such a tall stallion in a long time."

Nemesis agreed; the animal was beautiful and strong. The rest of her companions mounted their brown horses. They began to ride, and she leaned over her horse. "Alastor," she whispered.

"What?" Long Arm asked, riding by her side.

"I'm naming him Alastor," said Nemesis.

"That name rings a bell," said Edric in a deep voice.

"Legends say that the black horse of the God of War is called Alastor," John explained.

Long Arm cast a look towards Nemesis and whipped his mare's reins. The others followed suit and soon picked up speed, riding faster under the morning light.

Nemesis looked at John's back, her thoughts turning with concern. She couldn't trust him. She knew the men of this company wouldn't hesitate to betray her, or even kill her, if the need arose. She'd have to be careful.

They continued riding westward between tall trees with long branches. Nemesis was careful on her saddle, feeling the weight of her steel breastplate. She was the only one wearing armour, secretly jealous that her travelling companions weren't carrying the same weight. Although she never armoured her arms and legs in favour of mobility, the breastplate alone was enough to tire her out.

Alastor galloped for some time, and the trees started to get sparser before them. Nemesis recognised the road south of Oldlands' capital. Soon, they'd cross through plains and over hills, until they reached Long River. Her thoughts fleetingly wandered to her parents. Her father wouldn't be able to bear hearing that she'd chopped off a lord's manhood. He'd insist she should've found some other way to deter her potential rapist without hurting him, considering he was a rich noble. Perhaps he'd even tell her to allow him to take advantage of her, hoping that he'd marry her afterwards, and her mother would agree. Her mother had told her countless times how women weren't to question the rulings of the man of the house. Nemesis didn't think of her parents often, so every time she did, their memory triggered sadness. However ashamed she was to admit it, their death during the great plague that had swept the north years earlier had brought her some relief.

Nemesis had lost track of time as the sun set. The moon was almost ready to make its appearance. They'd been riding for a whole day, and their destination was two days away from Three Heads. She felt pain in her chest and shoulders from the weight of her breastplate, and hoped they'd soon stop to rest. *We don't have time to waste,* she told herself. They needed to ride on for as long as they could. They weren't even sure they'd find the Knight of the Moon where they were heading.

"Halt!" Long Arm called. "We have to stop, or we'll exhaust our horses."

Nemesis tugged on Alastor's reins and looked around. They were in a clearing, surrounded by sparse trees, with the moon and a few lonely stars visible above them. She led her steed to the nearest tree. The greenery around its roots seemed comfortable enough to lie on. Hopping off her horse, she tethered the reins to a small rock, and the three men near her followed her lead.

A little later, Nemesis was sitting on the ground on top of a small, woollen blanket with her steel breastplate placed to her right. Her companions ate bread and drank wine from their flasks while she ate the grapes and bits of cheese she'd brought with her.

"Are you sure you don't want any wine, my dear?" John offered.

Nemesis cast him a glare that could cut through rock. "We're not travelling across the kingdom for leisure, Long Arm. I would rather stay sober," she replied.

"Wine numbs the wits, soothing the mind. If you continue worrying about how we could die if we fail, we'll be doomed. A panicked mind is never healthy."

"I thought you were a bounty hunter, not a philosopher," Nemesis said.

"I've got many virtues, my dear."

Nemesis frowned. "I'd say you're a drunk who spends his coin on whores. Forgive me if I don't take your advice seriously."

John scoffed.

"Nobody's going to die," Alan held back a burp. "We'll catch that knight and bring his head to Gaeldeath's men."

"Even if we do fail, you're not in danger, Alan. Unfortunately, only my fame reached Walter's ears. Nemesis and I are the only ones who'll die, should we fail," said John.

Nemesis laughed dryly, and all three men looked at her. "Walter doesn't even know your name. He'd never be interested in a bounty hunter."

John seemed surprised. "But—the officers—"

"Gaeldeath's officers received orders to find Gareth without wasting men. Therefore, they looked for the best bounty hunter, and rumours lead to you. However, I doubt they bothered Walter with the details."

"Very well," said John, gulping wine from his flask.

"If the knight is near Long River, this will be easy work," said Alan restringing his bow.

"I'm not so sure. I've never faced a knight before," John replied.

"Between us, we'll best him," Edric insisted.

"You know the Knight of the Moon? Is he smart?" Alan asked Nemesis.

Nemesis nodded in agreement. Her mouth formed a grim line. "More still, he's very able with a sword."

"If he was smart, he wouldn't fall in love or care for marriage. He's lucky the knight's oath protected him from making decisions he'd regret," John replied with a laugh.

"I wouldn't expect anything more from a man that no woman would choose to lie with without payment," Nemesis told him.

John's smile didn't falter. "You'd be surprised if you knew how many women do choose my company, dear."

Nemesis snorted derisively. She didn't want to talk any more, she was tired.

"I thought that knights could marry," Edric spoke up.

"No. The law dictates that only if they are married before they take their oaths can they remain wedded, but then they are forbidden from having children," John explained.

Edric nodded silently.

"I think it's about time you stopped talking and let me sleep," Nemesis cut in.

She didn't want to speak anymore. The events of the last few days combined with her mission left her wallowing in rage and sadness. The truth was, she looked up to the Knight of the Moon, but she couldn't reject this assignment—she wasn't ready to die.

"Your wish is my command, my dear," John's voice rang out, and Nemesis laid down on her blanket over the moss. Her companions' snores soon reached her ears, but she remained awake until sunlight peeked over the horizon.

The Golden Hand

Nemesis watched the sky. Clouds adorned its overcast surface as they had often done during the past few days, but rain didn't seem to want to appear. She loved rain. When she watched the drops falling to the ground from the comfort of a window, she could feel her thoughts stilling.

She cast a glance at John, who was leading the way. They were crossing open plains, and dusk would soon fall.

"I've heard that Oldlands' villages have pretty women, but also the best wine in the kingdom," Alan said as he rode next to John and Edric.

"Vylor has the best women. That's why the convention of marriage isn't commonplace there. Smart thinking. With such beautiful women, why condemn yourself to spend your life with just one?" John mused.

"Who said that married men stay faithful to their woman?" Nemesis asked.

"In Tahos—the place I grew up—we honour marital traditions," Edric replied, looking back at her over his shoulder.

Nemesis laughed. "Marriage is an establishment made for the rich. A tradition so noble houses can unite, increasing their wealth. Most married men often visit brothels, and their wives have secret lovers."

"Not in Tahos," Edric insisted.

"Maybe..." Nemesis replied.

"I know what you mean," Long Arm cut in, turning his head towards her. "Though, there are many that try to honour their vows, believing in everlasting love." An ironic smile twitched his lips.

"If you love somebody, that's enough—marriage is a stupid formality."

John raised his flask, as if toasting her words. Nemesis watched him for a few moments. His thick, black hair was tousled with the wind, while his chestnut eyes had a strange vigour about them. She usually didn't like men like him, but in a strange way, John seemed smarter than most of his kind.

"The Knight of the Moon would disagree with you. From what I've heard, he wanted to marry Lady Alis—his love wasn't enough," said John.

"Men and women of noble birth often follow stupid traditions," Nemesis threw back.

"I thought you believed the Knight of the Moon to be smart," John pointed out.

Nemesis was tired of this conversation. "Wanting to marry doesn't make you stupid, Long Arm. I respect that man—I regret being tasked with killing him," she confessed.

"Why?" asked John.

Nemesis looked at him curiously.

"Why do you respect him?" John asked again.

"He is a man of honour."

Nemesis remembered Gareth smiling every time he saw her over the years. The knight often told her that she was one of the most able warriors he'd ever seen. Nemesis even admired him for loving Alis so much. She'd heard that he'd asked Robert Thorn to attaint him so he could marry Alis, but Gaeldeath's previous governor needed him, and Gareth decided to stay by his side.

"If you admire Gareth so much, why are you here trying to kill him?" asked Alan.

Nemesis turned to look at the man's face. "If I wasn't here, I'd be dead, idiot."

Alan brought his mare next to hers. His blue eyes were like still waters as he sized her up. His youthful face was thoughtful. "You could run away. You could go to the south and live far away from Gaeldeath under a different name. Nobody would ever find you."

"Gaeldeath is my home. I'm a warrior of the north. I won't hide away in the south, living like some village girl or working in a tavern," said Nemesis.

"You could fight for some southern governor," Alan suggested.

"That would be treason! I am a warrior of Tyverdawn's Guard. I know that words like honour and devotion aren't in the vocabulary of men such as you!" Nemesis' anger flared in her chest.

John spoke up. "I wonder where Gaeldeath's honour went when they decided to punish you because you killed your assailant. Where was the north's honour when they sent you to kill an innocent man? Gareth swore to always be by his governor's side, and he stood by that oath. If there was honour and devotion in Gaeldeath, Robert would still be governor and Walter would be dead or imprisoned for his crimes."

John's argument left Nemesis speechless. Her assumption that there was more to him than met the eye was true. Bounty hunters didn't usually think like this. This man was indeed interesting. "Why did *you* agree to kill a knight? Why didn't *you* run for the south?" she asked.

Long Arm pulled his horse's reins to slow it down. Nemesis on Alastor suddenly found herself riding by his side, and he faced her.

"My guess is you've never wandered far from the north—nobody pays for bounty hunters in the south. I'm the best at what I do, and I can only do it in the north."

Nemesis understood what he meant. People were capable of doing anything to avoid losing what gave their life meaning. Just as Nemesis was a warrior of the north, John was a bounty hunter.

"Why do they call him the Knight of the Moon?" asked Edric, the breeze ruffling his sparse hair.

"The emblem of his house is a crescent moon," John explained.

"I didn't expect you to know something like that," Nemesis said. John had surprised her again.

"I know more than you think," Long Arm replied with a smirk, his tone smug.

"I hope you know how to kill him, too. I've never hunted a knight before," Alan cut in.

"It won't be easy. Gareth was trained by Erneas." Nemesis had reflected on this fact many times already.

"I thought a member of the guard of Gaeldeath's capital would be more optimistic," John said.

Nemesis didn't speak for a few moments while Alastor shook his head. "I may belong to the City Guard, but I wasn't trained by a Grand Master."

"Brave, yet humble. I like it," Long Arm offered cheerfully. "The truth is, I prefer the knights of old. The current ones are quite dangerous."

"What do you mean?" Edric asked.

"Years ago, knights used to be like today's defenders. Many men that could use a sword were named knights, and they were given some land from nobles in exchange for loyalty. At some point, the rulers of the kingdom decided to give the knightly title only to the greatest of soldiers who formed their personal guard. From that point on, knights started to be trained only by Grand Masters," Nemesis explained.

Edric stayed silent, as if trying to process the information he'd just heard.

Dusk had started to fade into the darkness of the night. The clouds hid the stars in the sky, and Nemesis felt the weight of her breastplate wearing her down once more. They had been riding non-stop since first light, and they could now see the Iron Mountain. Nemesis hoped they'd reach their destination soon.

A faint light in the distance grabbed her attention. "I think I see something," she said.

Long Arm nodded sharply. "This is the first village near Long River."

As darkness spread around them, Nemesis could barely make out a handful of houses in the meagre light. A few men walked around. One of them seemed to notice Nemesis and the other three riders. The man started to run, and a few moments later, a dozen figures appeared in front of them; one of them holding a torch. John dismounted his mare and the others followed suit.

"Who are you?" a peasant demanded, taking a step forward.

"Travellers looking for lodgings."

The peasant pointed at Nemesis. "Why is that woman in armour?"

John laughed. "You know women. They're skittish. If we're attacked on the way, she wants to be ready."

Nemesis didn't like this comment. She considered women braver than men. However, she understood why John had said these words. Something inside her told her that he didn't actually believe them.

"Do I look like a half-wit to you?" the man shouted. "Steel ain't cheap. Where'd she get the gold to buy that fancy breastplate? You soldiers?"

Nemesis huffed. John had been right when he warned her that her armour would raise suspicion.

"We're merchants from the north, while Nemesis hopes to become a warrior," said John, looking at her. "We aren't rich, but occasionally, our wares fetch plenty of gold."

The peasant looked at John and Alan, then a moment later, regarded Edric's massive shape.

"What'd you want here?"

"To... We're looking for... Are there any merchants in this village?" asked John.

"Merchants?"

John nodded. "We run our business in the north, but we're thinking of selling goods in Oldlands, too. We're looking for a merchant to tell us about the area."

"The region's capital would be the best place to talk to merchants..."

"I've heard that one can find good-quality wares in the villages near Long River. Perhaps we can ask around here, and afterwards buy herbs and spices that would cost a lot more up north," John insisted.

"I thought you wanted to sell your own goods here in Oldlands."

"We've got a lot of plans," John answered plainly.

"We don't sell our crops to any merchants but our own!" the peasant replied.

"We both know that everything has a price." John threw a coin at the man, who caught it in one movement. He looked at John, then the coin.

Nemesis knew that while peasants gathered crops for their governors and the nobles of each region, they oftentimes sold a small portion to merchants, if the price was right.

"For the time being, we only want a place to stay the night, and to talk to a merchant," John went on.

The peasant hid the coin in his fist. "You're in luck. The Golden Hand is spending the night in the village."

"The Golden Hand?" John repeated.

"He's one of the most famous merchants in Oldlands. They call him that because he makes gold out of anything that falls into his hands."

John snorted derisively.

"Follow me," the peasant said a moment later.

The four companions followed the man and the other dozen peasants that had accompanied him, leading their horses behind them. Nemesis studied their surroundings. The houses were small with thatched roofs, while each was fenced in by a dozen wooden stakes. A little while later, they reached a modest stable and tied up their horses.

"You can spend the night in this stable. The Golden Hand is at the other end of the village. He's started a little fire, and he's roasting hares," said the peasant.

"Thank you. What's your name?" asked John.

"Tom," the man replied, and left with the other villagers.

John looked at Alan and Edric. "Stay here."

"I'll come with you," Nemesis told him.

"No," John said.

"Why?"

"We're looking for information. Merchants are distrustful, even if they talk a lot. We don't want Gareth to find out we're looking for him, if he's staying here. If this merchant deduces our reasons for being here, he could spread the news or hide what he knows. You don't know merchants and peasants well. You could say something that—"

"Take me with you, and I won't say a word," Nemesis said, cutting him off.

"Why do you want to come?"

"I want to witness your talent with my own eyes," she said. She tried to sound sarcastic but in reality, she wanted to hear what John would say to this man.

John huffed with frustration. "Take off the breastplate," he ordered.

Nemesis was enraged when men ordered her around. However, she obeyed, and a few moments later, she and John maneuvered through the small village until they found the fire. A man with a bony build sat next to it, roasting a hare tied to a stick above the flames.

"You must be The Golden Hand," said John. The firelight shadowed his face and glinted on the hilt of Nemesis' sword.

"That's yours truly," the merchant replied and turned towards them. "Who are you?"

"My name is John."

"And what do you want from me, John?"

"What is your real name?"

"Only my friends know my name, and you're not one of them. What do you want?" The Golden Hand insisted.

John frowned. "We're merchants too—from the north. We were thinking of buying a few goods from these villages to sell in the northern regions. We'd also like to sell a few northern spices in Oldlands' capital."

"It's the first time I've seen a merchant travelling with a woman by his side," said the man, his gaze pinned on Nemesis.

"She is an expert at haggling. If she's with you, you'll buy everything half price."

Beric studied her for a few moments, and she returned his gaze confidently. "And what do you want from me?"

"Information," John told him.

"There isn't any information, John. Any good merchant knows our job is based on two things: if you've got the gold, you can buy anything at a good price, and if you're smart, you can sell it at an even better one. When I started my trade, I didn't have enough gold to buy shoes, and now, I have a ship on the Silver Bay." The man's words were full of self-assuredness.

"What is the village with the best crops near Long River?" asked John.

"All of them are blessed with fertile soil! There are two more villages near the fringes of the Iron Mountain."

"Thank you," replied Long Arm.

"Now I'd like a little peace and quiet, John. I've got a few problems that I'm wondering if I can solve," the man said dryly.

"I know you just want to send me on my way. Any problem a man like you can have is easily solved."

The merchant looked at him curiously. "Why do you say that?"

"You said you have a ship. There's no problem you can't solve with a ship!"

The man stayed silent for a few moments before breaking into loud laughter. John started laughing too, while Nemesis looked at them, indignant.

"Beric," the man said after his laughter died down.

"Beric?" John repeated.

"My name is Beric. A man that can make me laugh like that deserves to be my friend."

John offered his hand, and Beric squeezed it.

"I suppose I'll see you often 'round these parts, then," Beric said.

John's smile didn't fade. "Of course. You've convinced me about the bounty of this land! I've heard that even knights visit the area."

Beric's face hardened. "Knights?"

"Yes... Many up north say that a knight of Gaeldeath comes here often when he wants to find a moment's peace. Gareth. I don't know if you've heard of him. Though, it could all just be rumours."

Nemesis was stunned with John's talent. He'd spoken these words so naturally that she was sure he hadn't aroused the faintest suspicion in Beric's mind.

"I've met a Gareth at a village a few miles south from here. It's the closest village to the Iron Mountain. I've got no idea if he was a knight, though!"

"What does it matter..." said John, indifferently. "Like I said, all of that could just be rumours, and that Gareth may just be a peasant with the same name."

Beric didn't speak, the crackling fire filling the stillness in the air.

"I think it's about time we left you alone," said John and nodded to Nemesis.

They left the firelight and headed back toward the stables. When they were far away enough, Nemesis glanced at John through the dark. "You've got skill," Nemesis told him.

"I know," he replied smugly, and Nemesis felt a desire to slap him. Self-assured men annoyed her. "That being said, we might have learnt nothing of real value. The Gareth he mentioned could really be a peasant." John added. Alan and Edric waited for them by the horses, glancing up as they approached.

"I doubt that. There are only three villages in the area. I don't think there are likely to be many Gareths," Nemesis replied.

"Maybe you should have asked the merchant if he knew the Knight of the Moon," said Edric, listening in to their conversation.

"You're an idiot," John said with a snort. "Gareth wouldn't want anyone to know his identity. I would imagine he introduces himself only by name."

"Perhaps he's going under a different name," Nemesis suggested and stroked Alastor's flank.

"Perhaps... We'll find out tomorrow. Even if we don't find him at that village, it won't take us too long to search all of them," John replied.

Nemesis nodded, taking a corner of the stable away from them. The others made themselves comfortable on the haybales and soon the sounds of snoring filled the darkness. Cloak wrapped around herself, Nemesis wondered how the Knight of the Moon would react when she stood before him.

The Forest of the Living Dead

John rode his mare carefully as they got closer to the village. Clouds hid the sun from view that morning. The previous night, his sleep had been fitful, leaving him exhausted. He knew that sooner or later they'd find the Knight of the Moon, and then, their mission would only get harder. A knight trained by a Grand Master was difficult prey.

John had thought it would be easier to kill Gareth with an arrow from afar. They would have to explore the village where the man lived without arousing suspicion, and then Alan would do what he did best. They surely didn't want to fight against a knight up close.

John cast a glance towards Edric, who was yawning atop his mare. *I'm worrying too much*, he told himself. Even in a melee, they'd be four against one. Although John and Alan weren't especially capable with a sword, they would be flanked by their massive companion and Nemesis, a guard of Tyverdawn.

John's thoughts strayed to Nemesis. He had told her to wait for them in a small patch of woods a few metres from the village. If they bumped into the Knight of the Moon, he would recognise her, which would land them all in hot water. For a moment, he turned his mind to Nemesis. Usually, he didn't like authoritative women, but there was something special about her. He had been astonished the moment he learned how she had punished the lord who had tried to rape her—*that showed rare courage.* He liked women with courage. He knew that Nemesis was brave and skilled with the sword; otherwise, the northerners would never have let her join the City Guard.

A silent voice spoke in his mind. *You like her. You've always liked brave women.* John tried to push away this thought. A woman like Nemesis would never choose a man like him. Sometimes, he felt that a small part of himself longed for a brave and courageous woman such as her. The idea that a lady like Nemesis could be interested in him made him feel special. However, he also knew that such fantasies rarely came true. There was no true love for him in this world. Sleeping with whores and numbing his mind with them was the best life—it led to no expectations and no disappointments about anything.

John saw a village to his left and he flicked his horse's reins. Alan and Edric followed suit. They rode across open plains lush with grass and dotted with a few trees. Fortunately, the village they had spent the previous night in was only a few miles away, so it didn't take long to reach their destination. He saw two men dragging large carts loaded with wheat while a handful of small houses came into view in the distance.

John slowed his horse. A creek of the Long River ran by the small village. Nearby, a dozen men were cutting wood. A woman riding a donkey made her way towards them. Alan turned his mount to allow her to pass, and John studied her suspicious gaze as she watched them.

"Who are you?" a voice demanded. A stubby, fat man from the group cutting wood made his way towards them, carrying an axe.

"Merchants from the north," John replied sharply.

"From the north? No merchant from the north has come here before."

"We've heard this village has grain, herbs, and the best spices in the kingdom."

"We don't sell our crops to foreign merchants. Our crops belong to Oldlands."

John brought out a pouch and dangled it in front of the man's face. "Here's three hundred gold pieces. You sure you don't want to do business with us?"

The man looked at the pouch, then John. He didn't seem moved by the gold.

"Can I speak to Gareth?" asked John.

The man's face dropped, panic settling across his features upon hearing his words. John could have sworn he saw him raise his axe by a few centimetres.

"What do you need from me?" another voice came.

John turned to see a tall, well-built man of around forty with thick chestnut hair. His clothes were tattered, and he too carried an axe.

"I stopped at a village a few miles down and a merchant told me this place has the best wares, and that Gareth is the right man to talk to."

"Which merchant?" Gareth asked.

"He didn't tell me his name." John was careful not to reveal too much and risk exposing his lie. The village they'd come from was so close by that he was sure everybody knew each other.

"Whoever told you that was wrong. I'm only good at chopping logs and dragging carts," Gareth threw back. His eyes were hazel and there was a thin scar just above his right eyebrow.

John looked at the man carefully. He couldn't tell if he was the knight they were looking for.

"As I said before, we don't deal with merchants from other areas. I'm sure you'd have better luck with the other villages near Long River," the stubby man spoke again.

"I'm disappointed we won't be doing business together," John said, and he returned his pouch to his belt.

With a nod, John rode off with Alan and Edric following behind.

•◦•

Nemesis chewed on a piece of bread, her mind restless with all that John had reported. John, Alan and Edric nibbled on a bit of cheese and a few figs. Their horses were tied a few metres away, and she could make out Alastor's back as he grazed.

"You're sure that this man is the Gareth we're looking for?" asked Alan once more.

"If you ask again, I'll bury my sword in your eye," Nemesis said through a mouthful. She'd told them at least four times that the man they had described was surely the Knight of the Moon.

Nemesis kept on eating while she tried to plan what to do next. It'd be very difficult to kill Gareth. "We need to find a way to get him out of that village," she said, swallowing.

"I know," John replied, quieter than usual. "Though, I wonder how…"

"I hope he doesn't run away with his lady. Maybe he suspected we are not merchants but soldiers who want his head," said Edric.

"I doubt it. There are only four of us and he is a knight. He won't leave because of us," John replied.

"I still think there's some way we can quietly get rid of him while he's still in the village," said Alan.

Nemesis felt enraged. Alan had to be exceptionally slow. "How? You said that the peasants seemed to want to protect him, and there's no way we can go unnoticed in that village. There aren't many trees near the houses, only open plains. We can't get within shooting range, so arrows would be useless, and if we try and engage in close combat, the peasants will back him up. We'd need thirty armed men to overwhelm them."

Alan opened his mouth to say something, then closed it again with an annoyed look. Nemesis wanted to punch him; she was tired of explaining the same thing over and over.

"We need to find a clever way to lure him out here. This thicket is perfect for hiding and for Alan to kill him with an arrow," John spoke.

"We can try, but it won't be easy," Nemesis replied.

"I have to think about it." John hadn't drunk a drop of wine that night—a worrying sign. "I'll try to sleep, and we'll talk about it in the morning."

Nemesis wanted to think too, without listening to Alan's nonsense. They finished eating in silence, and Nemesis laid down on the blanket she'd put on the ground. A few moments later, her gaze fell on the nearest tree. Its branches had yellow-green leaves that were long and thin. She had seen a similar tree in the Forest of Tears when she was still a little girl. Her father had taken her along on one of his travels to Eryn Bay, and their journey brought them to the forest. Nemesis had been terrified, and she had confessed this fear to her father who had only scared her more.

"Many know the Forest of Tears as the Forest of the Living Dead. Some legends say that the dead come to life in this place, and take on strange forms, cursing any living traveller they find in their way."

Her father had never tried to soothe her in his life. He always wanted to fill her with fear and guilt—guilt for not wanting to follow his bidding.

She looked away from the tree and towards the steel breastplate and sword next to her. A dragging sound made her raise her head, and she grabbed the hilt of her sword with her right hand.

"It's me!" John had approached her.

"You scared me!" Nemesis's heart was still beating fast.

"You can't sleep?"

Nemesis raised her body from her blanket. "No."

"What were you thinking about?" asked the man.

She wasn't sure why he was speaking to her. "My father", she confided.

"Let me guess," John sat next to her with slow movements. "He never wanted you to become a soldier... He only wanted to wed you to a rich prick and gain power."

Nemesis was astonished. "Why do you say that?"

"Every father with a daughter as beautiful as you are hopes for the same..."

"You know too much for a bounty hunter," *Probably more than any of them.*

Long Arm smiled. "Your father is an idiot."

Nemesis frowned. "Is that sarcasm?"

The smile didn't fade from the man's lips. "No. You are a brave woman. Braver than many idiot soldiers in the north. In my thirty years in this world, I have never met one I liked."

She wasn't used of men saying these words. "How do you know I am brave?"

John scoffed. "You are from the north! A place where most men never respect women. If you had the courage to become a member of Tyver-dawn's Guard and defy every tradition, you are brave."

Nemesis felt awkward. This was one of the best things she had heard in the twenty-three years of her life. Yet, she never thought she would hear it from a bounty hunter.

"You shouldn't be here looking for this knight with us. Not because you killed that scum... I shouldn't be here either. They sent us to kill a man who was loyal to his true ruler," John said.

"You are a bounty hunter. I thought men in your business could not allow themselves to care about anything."

John frowned. "Bounty hunters chase thieves and merchants who owe money. They do not get hired to kill knights. This man, Gareth, seems to be a man of honour. Few soldiers stay loyal to their leader when everyone else turns their back on them."

"He is a man of honour. A man who only wanted to serve his ruler and be with the woman he loved."

"I don't know about love," John said.

"You never truly loved someone?" Nemesis asked.

"No. And nobody ever loved me. Love is a fairytale."

Nemesis caught his tone and watched his face. His eyes opened and closed fast as he said his words. He seemed nervous as if he was hiding something. "I don't think you truly believe that. I think deep inside you, you wish someone loved you... You just say that love doesn't exist because you are scared that no one will ever love you... Or you are afraid that there might be someone who says she loves you and then betrays you. It's easier to pretend love doesn't exist than face your own fears."

John seemed puzzled. He opened his mouth to speak when a noise made them both turn. Nemesis grabbed the hilt of her blade again.

"I'd advise you to leave that sword."

Nemesis looked up and saw a group of men surrounding her and John and their sleeping companions, holding axes. A small furrow formed on the forehead of the Knight of the Moon as he looked down at her with glowing eyes.

Gaeldeath's Honour

John couldn't believe they had been caught. He walked behind Edric and Alan, stealing glances towards Nemesis on his right. He couldn't understand how they'd blown their cover.

They kept marching until John saw the village they had visited that morning. *They probably plan to kill us. I'd have never expected to die in a place like this.* He looked for a means of escape, but there was nothing. The peasants had surrounded them wielding axes, and what's more, they'd taken their horses.

John and his companions were ushered into the village, and they saw quite a few women staring at them from the doors of their wooden houses. They seemed unsettled by the unwelcome visitors who had been captured near their land. John had tried to explain to the villagers and the knight that they were only merchants who had decided to spend the night in the forest, but his lies were foolish since Gareth knew Nemesis.

As they walked a little further, John realised they were being led to a barn. Two horses grazed by its corner. That, then, was to be his end. He would die in a stable, surrounded by manure.

The villagers tied up his horse and the other three and ordered them to head to a corner of the stable. Then Gareth nodded sharply, and the men that had escorted them there began to leave. Just one villager remained by the knight's side, while a woman rushed into the barn. Her hair was straight, golden-coloured, while her eyes were a dark shade of blue.

"Is that them?" she asked.

Gareth glanced at her. "Yes."

"Nemesis?" the woman exclaimed with a look of surprise.

"Good evening, Alis," Nemesis said.

"What are you doing here?"

"It's obvious. Walter sent her to kill me," said Gareth.

John watched Nemesis. She looked ashamed.

"I may have left Tyverdawn, but the news still reached my ears... I was still in Gaeldeath when I learned that Nemesis killed a noble. I heard that Walter wanted to have her executed, though many officers, as well as Erneas, opposed that. Walter doesn't want any more discord in his region these days, so they agreed on a punishment. I didn't find out what it was, though now I know... I never expected that they would punish her by sending her to kill me, but that must be the reason she is here."

"Gareth—" Nemesis began.

"I'm sure you didn't mention any of this to Erneas before leaving Gaeldeath. He'd be ashamed of you if he were to find out what you were doing," Gareth interrupted Nemesis angrily.

John wanted to shout that they didn't care what Gaeldeath's Grand Master would feel. He wanted to get it over with. The anticipation of his coming death made his stomach churn.

"I didn't have any choice," said Nemesis, shame colouring her tone.

"That's not true. You could have left Walter—you could have left the north," Alis said with a confident tone.

"And where would I go? I'm a warrior of Gaeldeath. If I took refuge in another city, I'd have to become a washerwoman or a cook! I'd never fight for any army or guard that didn't belong to Gaeldeath. I swore it so when I joined Tyverdawn's Guard!" Nemesis raised her voice.

"You swore? Nobody in Gaeldeath has honour. The people of this region trampled their oaths towards Robert Thorn, and you want to honour your oath by killing in Walter's name!" Gareth's face reddened with anger.

The knight approached them, and John noticed a sword hanging from his belt—the sword that would soon take his life.

"These here are bounty hunters?" the knight asked.

Nemesis nodded.

"I'd expect that Walter would put a bounty on me, although I didn't expect he'd send you to kill me... That man has no honour." Gareth's eyes shifted to John. "How did you find me?"

"It wasn't that difficult, my lord. The men who set me on this mission knew that you've been visiting Lady Alis for a while now at a village near the Iron Mountain." John had decided to tell the truth. After all, his end was near.

Gareth didn't seem to expect those words. "They knew? They knew I was coming here? Few know this secret."

"Apparently that is not the case," said John.

"No secret remains hidden in Tyverdawn..." Nemesis spoke.

Gareth shot her a look.

"Sir Gareth," John raised his voice, and the knight turned to him once more. "I have a question for you, and since we're to die soon, I'd like you to honour me with the truth."

Gareth stayed silent.

"How did you discover our reason for being here? Did you suspect us when we met this morning?"

The knight laughed. "You tried to fool the wrong man. The Golden Hand told me that someone was looking for me, pretending he was a merchant... He asked for gold for his information. I hope your idiocy didn't convince him I was actually a knight, as nobody outside this village knows that secret."

In his mind's eye, John saw Beric's scrawny form. He hoped to stay alive so he could take his head. His eyes fell on Alan and Edric on his left. Their faces were contorted with the fear of death.

Gareth stayed silent for a few more moments, bringing his hand to his chin. John's gaze flickered to Nemesis. There wasn't the faintest trace of fear in her black eyes, only that familiar anger. John couldn't help but admire her for that.

"Do what you have to, Gareth," said Nemesis, raising her voice.

The Knight of the Moon's face was painted with a faint smile.

The Oath of Love

"I will give you a choice," said Gareth. "I've taken many lives in my years, but I've grown tired of killing... If you swear to me that you will leave here and never return, I'll grace you with your life. If, however, you don't honour your oath and I find you on this land again, I will take your heads."

Nemesis didn't believe his words.

"You don't understand, Gareth. The men that ordered me to kill you want your head, whatever it takes. Walter won't rest until you're punished. Even if we fail, he'll send others after you" John insisted.

"I'm not afraid of Walter," rebuked the knight.

"If we fail to kill you, he will increase the bounty and then every mercenary will be looking for you!" John raised his voice.

"I'll find a way to deal with Walter and his men if needed. However, you need to decide whether you choose to leave here once and for all, or die."

John studied Gareth. "I never wanted this job. Gaeldeath's men discovered I'm the best bounty hunter in the north and forced me to take on this mission. My companions"—he looked at Edric and Alan—"are unknown by the soldiers that sent me. But, these men told me that if Nemesis and I don't return with your head within ten days, they'd put a bounty on us, too. We have only six days left."

"So, you decided to kill me and continue your business..." said the knight. "The only solution is to leave for the south. Hide in a village or a distant city."

"I thought about making a run for the south, but there isn't a place for bounty hunters there..." John said.

"I don't care if you have to stop being a bounty hunter, or if you"—his gaze turned towards Nemesis—"have to become a washer woman for some lord. I'm sure that sooner or later, Walter and your pursuers will forget about you. If you don't swear you'll leave this place forever, you'll die. No chore, no humiliation is excuse enough to take orders from a man like Walter."

"If you hate Walter so much, why are you here, Gareth?" Nemesis spoke up.

"What do you mean?"

"Why didn't you ride with Robert to Iovbridge? Why aren't you fighting by the side of the governor *you've* sworn your faith to? I'm sure that Robert won't leave his son's treachery unpunished, and the Royal Army will fight by his side," Nemesis had been pondering this question for a long time.

Gareth's gaze grew distant and Alis touched his hand. "Lord Robert has relieved me of my duties."

"Even if he did, you could have refused! You swore to fight by his side, and now that his own son has stained his honour, you left him. The rest of the knights of Gaeldeath, your sworn brothers, are dead! You speak of *my* honour and the honour of a few mercenaries, but you're not by Robert's side when he needs you more than ever."

"Enough!" Gareth shouted. "You are a guard of Gaeldeath's capital, Nemesis. Your oath demands you protect your governor until his final moments, and even so you have become Walter's slave. You too could have headed for the south to fight for Robert."

"My oath is towards Gaeldeath. It would be treachery to fight for a southern army, even by Robert's side. However, I thought a knight's oath was more significant than any other. It demands you sacrifice yourself for your governor, and you allowed Robert to cast you aside!" Nemesis knew she went too far. Her words could lead to her execution.

Gareth's expression changed, and he looked away. This wasn't anger, but guilt. The knight stretched his hand towards Alis. She took it and rested her head on his shoulder.

"When I took the knight's oath, I was ready to stand by every word. Yet, when I met Alis, everything changed. I felt for the first time that no oath, no governor and no war had significance. I wanted to marry her and start a family. I wanted to live far away from the politics and backstabbing of the kingdom." Gareth paused for a moment.

"Robert knew this... However, he couldn't relieve me of my oath while I was still young. A gesture like that would raise questions, and if the truth was discovered, my honour would be stained as well as Robert's reputation; nobles who already considered him a spineless governor would have their opinions confirmed. Therefore, he let me take some days off every few months to visit Alis here. This is where she ran to when her parents imposed an arranged marriage to a rich lord upon her."

"When Robert lost Gaeldeath and prepared to travel to the south, I asked to go with him. He smiled at me and told me I was free to follow my heart's true desire... Robert Thorn is a virtuous man. I considered disobeying him, considered fighting by his side," Gareth spoke again.

"Why didn't you?" Nemesis asked.

"As you said, Robert doesn't want to leave Walter unpunished. Along with the king, they will mobilise their armies in the north, and I don't want to die for the sake of land and wealth. I don't want to fight in cities that will be pillaged and see women violated to their last breath. I want to live by Alis' side, and if love drives me to my death, I prefer to die for her than for the title and land of a lord," the knight cast a longing look at Alis.

Nemesis had never heard words like these from a man before. They moved her—gave her hope. Perhaps in the end there were men that could lead the kingdom towards a better future.

"I will not try to harm you again, Sir Gareth Huneywood—even if it costs me my life." Nemesis bent her head, then bowed deeply to the knight in front of her.

Power and Honour

Nemesis watched the open plains and clear skies from a corner of the village, her thoughts restless. She hadn't slept the previous night, the words of the Knight of the Moon resurfacing in her mind.

"I want to live by Alis' side, and if love drives me to my death, I prefer to die for her than for the title and land of a lord."

Those were some of the most beautiful words she'd ever heard in her life. She remembered her father telling her that love was a fairytale for children, and how wealth and power were the only things of value in life. She knew that most men in Gaeldeath agreed with him, and it saddened her.

Nemesis saw a bird with yellow and red plumes flying overhead, chirping. Sometimes, she dreamt she could fly too, and go somewhere far from the north—some place where the people were better than those of Gaeldeath. Erneas had told her that in some southern regions, people had honour and values, something that was rare in the place she had grown up. This gave her hope for the human race. Still, however appealing the south seemed, she couldn't betray her homeland.

"I thought that you and the bounty hunters would be gone by dawn."

Nemesis saw Gareth standing next to her. "We've been riding for three days. We planned on resting a little and leaving soon after dusk," she said.

Gareth sat on the grass next to her. "Erneas always said you were special. He was disappointed that due to some idiotic traditions he couldn't train you."

"Did you come here to tell me he'd be disappointed in me if he found out what I did? Perhaps he knows already... I'm sure that everyone who argued against my hanging has learned of my mission... Otherwise, they would think I'm dead, and as you said, Walter doesn't need any more discord in Gaeldeath."

"I think that Erneas was right. I know how love for our land often leads to stupid decisions. In Gaeldeath, men and women have been raised for centuries to put their land above all else. They teach us to ignore every action of our superiors, every order that is against our honour, shouting that we must do everything for our fatherland," Gareth huffed. "I was once like you, Nemesis. However, I now know what I must do."

Nemesis looked him straight in the eyes. "Do you think I'm special?"

The man nodded.

"Why?"

"When I told you I now want to only fight for love, I saw the spark in your eyes. I saw that deep down, you know what I've come to understand with time. I'm sure that you don't truly wish to fight by the side of a man like Walter. A man who didn't applaud what you did to your assailant, but punished you, and sent you to kill an innocent knight."

Nemesis sighed. "Walter won't forget... We are two warriors of the north. He and his men will hunt us down for years," she said.

"Walter doesn't only seek to control Gaeldeath. I heard his ambition is to sit on Knightdorn's throne—the throne his grandfather built. I'm sure that his aspirations will overtake his desire for revenge," the man said, his tone firm. "If you want, you can stay here."

Nemesis didn't expect to hear these words. "You honour me with your trust after all I've done. Though, a village is no place for me."

"If I was younger, perhaps I'd say the same. Yet, I believe life here will make you understand that peace and serenity are far greater than battles and war. What's more, if you stay, I'll train you. I'll teach you everything Erneas taught me."

Nemesis' eyes shot wide open. "You tell me to seek peace while offering to teach me the secrets of battle—secrets that can make me an even more dangerous warrior?"

"You can use power however you want, Nemesis. If I teach you all I know, perhaps you'll use that knowledge and skill to kill innocents and grow your power and wealth. Perhaps, though, you could choose to use it to build a better world. The choice would be yours."

Tears welled up in her eyes. "Why do you trust me?"

"You remind me of myself. Maybe I can help you forget your rage and see what else there is to life. Think about it."

Gareth smiled, then stood up slowly and left. Nemesis watched him walk away, more moved than ever.

⸻◈⸻

John couldn't believe all that Nemesis had told him. "Do you have a deathwish?" he shouted, his voice filling the small stable.

Nemesis seemed surprised. "Since when do you care about me, Long Arm?"

John didn't know how to reply to that. "I wouldn't want any of my companions to die," he told her.

"Since when am I your companion?" Nemesis spat.

"We've travelled together. I've learned things about you... It's my duty to... If you stay here, you'll die," He had to change her mind. He didn't want her to get harmed. He knew that it was easier not to care about anybody but he couldn't help it right now.

"I never expected to hear the word *duty* from a man like you."

John huffed angrily, arms crossed over his chest. That's why he didn't give a damn about others. When he let himself care, nobody ever respected him.

"Thank you," said Nemesis after a moment, and she seemed to mean it. "Though, maybe life here is what I've been looking for all these years." Her tone was soft.

"Life in a village?"

She stared out at the houses, her dark eyes losing some of their glint. "Yes... maybe here, where nobody cares for glory and power, I could earn more respect than I ever did in Gaeldeath."

"Peasants have even less respect for women than people who live in cities."

"I'm sure that doesn't apply to this place."

John rested his hands on his waist, annoyed. "Find another village like this. You'll die here! Walter's men might not bother too much with me, but you and Gareth are in danger."

"I trust Gareth. I'm sure he knows what he's doing. If bounty hunters or soldiers come here, we'll hide until they leave. On top of that, I'll learn the art of battle from a knight!" Nemesis insisted.

"No martial skill will be of any use to you if you're dead! You think I am the only man able to get hold of information? Every mercenary in the north will make it their life's purpose to find you with such a high reward. Do you know what will happen to this village if every bounty hunter in the north flocks here?"

Nemesis looked at him, waiting for him to continue.

"They'll ravage every woman, kill every man and child, and keep you as a plaything for weeks before they kill you."

"I've made my decision."

John's gaze became distant and he sat in a corner of the stable on a pile of hay. The thought of her dying filled him with sorrow. He didn't understand why he was feeling this way, but he knew he had to try harder to change her mind.

"You look sad... I never expected you to care so much about me," Nemesis said, looking at him. A smile had formed on her lips. It was the first time he had seen her express gratitude. John felt the impulse to say something but he didn't have the courage.

"It's good to know that you care about something other than yourself," Nemesis said.

John raised his gaze. "I do care about the people I like. I care about

Alan and Edric. I care about… you."

Nemesis frowned. "Why do you like me?"

"You are a brave woman. You are…" he cut mid-sentence—he wouldn't say more. He knew she would reject him and that would fill his heart with sadness. *I shouldn't have said all this.*

"I am?" Nemesis said.

"You are a brave woman with honour. Those are rare qualities in the kingdom," John said.

"Where are Alan and Edric?" Nemesis asked. She was staring at him, puzzled, as if she could tell there were more things John wanted to say, but he couldn't.

"They heard that east of the village there is a large patch of Eye of the Sun growing, and they set out to look for it. They'll be back soon. I told them that we should leave before nightfall and the sun has almost set."

"Eye of the Sun?" she repeated, brow furrowed.

"It's the best plant to smoke."

She frowned, rolling her eyes.

"It's a shame there's no other knight elsewhere to train you," said John.

Nemesis came over and sat next to him. "Knights and Grand Masters don't train women, Long Arm."

"Because they're idiots," John replied.

"Only a few believe that women could become worthy warriors." The features of Nemesis' face seemed to soften.

"Because people are stupid! The legends and traditions of this Kingdom are only for fools. I've travelled the world and I've seen knights and great warriors scream and whimper when facing death. When we got caught, I saw your eyes. There was no fear. You were ready to die bravely for your beliefs. That, I would say, is the highest virtue of a knight—a virtue that can't be taught, but is granted at birth. If I was a Grand Master, I'd have surely picked you for an apprentice."

Nemesis didn't speak and she walked towards him slowly. "Do you really believe that?"

John nodded. "I admired you when we were at Gareth's mercy. No man has your coura—"

John didn't manage to finish his sentence before Nemesis had grabbed him by the shoulders. She faced him, and he saw her eyes sizing him up with unexpected lust. Their lips joined passionately, and the woman pushed him back onto the hay. John let himself drop, fumbling with his belt, while Nemesis swiftly threw off her clothes with abandon. She climbed on top of him, her expression full of need. John stroked her breasts and thrust inside her as she moved against him. He felt her nails pressing into his flesh. He caressed her hardened nipples as her body moved more urgently on his manhood. His fingers slipped below her waist, and he squeezed her skin as she let out a moan. Their rough tryst continued for a while, their laboured breathing the only sound that broke the silence inside the small barn until their joint exclamations of satisfaction could be heard.

The Mercernary's Decision

"I'll stay," said Nemesis, watching as rays of light fell across Gareth's face.

The man smiled. "Are you sure?"

Nemesis nodded, although a trace of doubt had appeared in her mind. Even if the knight wanted to teach her all he knew, the conversation she had had the previous night disturbed her constantly. "John believes that Walter's men will find us here. He didn't struggle to track you down."

"I didn't expect you'd take a bounty hunter seriously."

Nemesis stayed silent. She didn't believe that she'd take a man like John seriously either. "John is not like most of the bounty hunters you know. He is smart… He is…", she paused mid-sentence. She was confused. "Walter's men have heard the rumours. They know that you're in this region. If just a few men are sent after you, someone like the Golden Hand will direct them straight to you," she said.

"I know." Gareth brought a hand to his chin. "So far, nobody around these parts has ever learned the truth about me. Everyone I've met is under the impression that I'm a villager that occasionally leaves to bring crops to merchants. Only here do they know my real identity. Though, if more and more men come looking for me, it will arouse the suspicion of villagers and travelling merchants from surrounding villages. Some are willing to do anything for a little gold."

"So, we can't stay here."

"I have a plan," said Gareth, his voice coloured by hesitancy. "I didn't want to tell you until you'd decided if you're going to stay here, but I think I can trust you now."

"I swear I won't try to hurt you again, Gareth. I swear on my honour. I regret agreeing to kill you," Nemesis said, and she meant every word.

"I'll tell you everything, but if you betray me, you will die like a dog. Alis' life depends on this secret," Gareth said, all traces of his smile gone.

Nemesis looked at him with determination.

"For some time, the people of this village have been building a few houses on a side of the Iron Mountain. In three days, Alis and I will move there along with a dozen villagers," said the man.

"You'll live on the Iron Mountain? Why there?"

Gareth nodded. "The earth of that area is quite fertile. The villagers that will remain here will send us supplies, while no one else will know where we went."

"You trust these people that much?"

The knight nodded. "I trust them with my life. No one in this village betrayed my identity as a knight all these years. The secret is safe with them."

"Why take villagers with you? You could go there alone with Alis."

Gareth frowned. "The area is full of ahronth, a rare and precious plant that acts as an antidote for many poisons. Lords of Oldlands as well as many merchants have been after it for a while, but it's a long and arduous journey there and back in one day, with harvesting the plant in between. By living near the site of the ahronth the villagers would be able to harvest a much larger amount more easily. The people that would come with us would help with harvesting the ahronth."

"And you'll bring the herbs here afterwards?"

The man nodded. "That won't be difficult. A villager from either here or the new settlement will take on that job. This way, we will be kept safe while also helping the village earn a little more gold."

Nemesis considered the plan for a few moments. "Is there a house for me on the mountainside?"

Gareth smiled. "Only if you promise to help with the ahronth harvest during your stay."

Nemesis returned his smile.

"The bounty hunters should leave before us—nobody else should know this secret. I thought they would have left last night."

Nemesis felt a strange weight in her chest and her grin faded. "If you agree, they'd like to stay for a day more," she said.

"If you promise they will only stay for one more day, it's fine," Gareth said. "Now, if you'll excuse me. I need to find Alis." The man turned around and left.

Nemesis watched the clear sky while the scorching sun bathed the small village with its morning light. A few men worked while women carried wooden pitchers filled with water from the Long River. This place was strangely peaceful, filled with a kind of serenity she couldn't remember feeling before. However, she knew that soon she would feel pain squeezing her heart. John's words the previous night had made her feel special—even though she knew the truth. Men like him couldn't truly love easily. Love and passion scared them. Soon, John would leave, and a strange bitterness filled her every time she thought about it.

It was just one night, she told herself. She was left looking at the village landscape for a few moments, until she felt a strange urge—an urge to try and keep John by her side.

<hr>

John stole a shy glance towards Nemesis and lowered his gaze. He wasn't good at words—at least not the ones needed for this situation. He couldn't remember having feelings like this for someone before.

"I was looking for you for some time," said Nemesis after a moment.

"Edric and Alan insisted we head south this morning—they told me we could find precious metals near the fringes of the Iron Mountain, though we found nothing. We returned to rest, and soon we'll leave this village once and for all." The last sentence came out as a whisper.

John had expected Nemesis to want to talk to him that morning. After the events of the previous night, she had gone to sleep, while he'd woken up when Edric and Alan came back. His companions had found them dressed, and hadn't the faintest suspicion of what had happened between them. He had encouraged them to fall asleep and leave the village the following day. When the sun had risen, John had decided to travel with them for a few hours before Nemesis woke up. He needed to avoid her and think.

He glanced towards her again. Her black eyes held a strange expression. It was not rage, nor passion. It looked like something he had never seen in the depths of her irises before—something he couldn't explain. John had thought about exactly what he'd tell her when he saw her, though it was as if his thoughts had evaporated.

"You don't have anything to say to me?" Nemesis asked.

John felt an unfamiliar unease. "I don't know what to say," he admitted.

"Look at me."

John lifted his gaze sheepishly, like a boy who had been caught misbehaving.

"I don't want you to leave. I want you to stay here with me."

John couldn't believe his ears. "I don't know why you'd say something like that. No woman wants a man like me."

John wondered about the meaning of what he had just said; he didn't know how he truly felt. Did his words mean that he couldn't stay faithful to a woman, or did he feel he didn't deserve a woman like Nemesis?

"I think you're afraid."

John looked Nemesis in the eye, her words digging into him. "Afraid? Afraid of what?" he asked, his jaw set.

"I've met many men whose only purpose had been finding young and beautiful whores to sleep with every day. Men who care only for gold and the mindless pleasure of prostitutes. However, no matter how much you want to seem like them, you're not."

John chuckled. "You know nothing about me... Whatever happened last night was—"

John stuttered. He didn't know how to finish his sentence while Nemesis waited to see where he was going with it.

"I'll never become a man like Gareth. You're wrong about me. I'm just a bounty hunter who seeks gold and young women to keep him company."

Nemesis broke into a smile much to his disbelief.

"I told you again the night that Gareth caught us. You are scared... You want everyone to believe you're like that because you're afraid."

"What are you saying?"

"Men who only care about gold and women aren't interested in knights or their stories, nor the traditions of the kingdom. You are a man with curiosity, who constantly seeks out the truth. You know how to read people better than anyone. However, you're afraid. You're afraid that if one day people discover who you truly are, you will be hurt. You want to be like the rest of the men of your profession. But you aren't... and I know the truth."

"Have you lost your mind? Until yesterday you thought I was just a lech who spends his time in taverns and brothels... Now you think I'm something more? I wonder why you'd want a man like me."

Nemesis remained quiet for a moment. "I knew there was more to you and I was right," she said, their eyes meeting.

"You tried to understand me from the start—to see the truth in my gaze—and you did. You saw who I truly am. I think you want to stay with me too, John, but you're scared. You're afraid that maybe you don't deserve a woman like me. You're afraid that one day, I'll discover that very fact and leave you. You've lived for almost thirty years, but you're a coward."

Her words had paralysed him. It was the first time a woman had seen so much in him; the first time a woman had understood how he felt. He wanted Nemesis more than anything he had ever wanted in his life, but he didn't want to admit it to himself. He could swear that someone like her had no use for a man like him.

"Don't be a coward, John."

He liked it every time she said his name. John didn't know what to do, until a surge of courage flooded him. Then, he bent towards Nemesis and kissed her. "I'll stay."

He almost didn't believe the words he uttered came from him. It was the first time he had allowed himself to put all his fears aside—the first time he had felt that perhaps he didn't have to spend the rest of his life alone.

The Iron Mountain

John was lost in his thoughts as he walked, shooting glances towards Edric and Alan who were leading their horses alongside him. His companions had spent five whole days in the village, and the time had come to start their journey back. Gareth was initially irritated when John asked to stay for that long. Gareth didn't trust him; he was worried that John might betray him, although he changed his mind when Nemesis assured him that the mercenaries were of no danger to him.

John continued watching the two men. They planned to return to Three Heads since Walter's soldiers didn't pose a threat to them. Alan and Edric had decided to make use of the hospitality and peace of mind provided by Gareth's village, but now they would have to part ways. His companions weren't ready to live a life away from adventure and gold. Even if they wanted to, Gareth wouldn't allow them to join the others on their journey to the Iron Mountain, and had ordered John not to divulge their plan or their destination.

He remembered Alan's expression the moment he'd told them that he planned to stay at the village.

"You'll stay here?" Alan had asked, wide-eyed.

"Only for a little while. That way, I'll avoid Walter's men who'll be looking for me at Three Heads."

"And you decided to stay here with a man wanted dead by Walter?"

"I won't stay here for long. Soon, I'll head for the south."

"Why did you decide that?" Alan had asked.

"What choice do I have? We can't kill a knight."

Alan had burst into laughter. "*Do you take me for an idiot? The John I knew would have found a thousand ways to kill a target for that much gold. I know something is going on between you and Nemesis. I've seen how you look at each other... Finally, a woman managed to charm you, Long Arm.*"

John hadn't expected Alan to have caught on.

"Time to say our goodbyes," Edric's voice rang out.

John smiled at him. The giant man trundled towards him and wrapped his arms around him. Immediately afterwards, he mounted his horse. Alan moved to hug John, too.

"Until next time, old friend," said Alan. "If you ever feel like returning to your old ways, you know where to find us."

"Perhaps one day, we'll spend the night again in a northern tavern," John said sorrowfully.

Alan nodded and jumped on the back of his horse. The two men cast him one last look before setting off swiftly. A strange fear came upon John, not because he was leaving the life of a bounty hunter behind, but because he felt no regret in doing so. He was filled with longing every time he pictured spending the rest of his life with Nemesis. Though, that was also the thing that scared him. It was the first time he had felt like this—the first time he was willing to leave everything behind for a person. He shuddered at the idea of something going wrong and one day Nemesis deciding he wasn't the man she was looking for.

John stayed for a few moments to watch his former companions' horses get smaller in the distance, then he took a deep breath and headed for the stable. Soon, the journey towards their new home would begin.

Nemesis looked at the morning sun bathing the tips of the Iron Mountain in golden light while Alastor trotted at a leisurely pace. She didn't know how long it would take them to reach their destination. Turning, she looked at John who rode on her left. His decision to stay with her had moved her. She knew full well that for a man like him, it wasn't an easy decision to make. Frankly, she had never expected to convince him to stick with her, and yet here he was.

She remembered not liking John from the moment she'd laid eyes on him. He had seemed like one of the countless drunks she had met in the north. Whores, ale, and wine were the only companions of men like that, and Nemesis felt only disgust when she came across them. However, John had proved himself to be different. Of course, he had certainly spent a good few years of his life drinking and laying with prostitutes, but there was more to him than that. John respected women. He wasn't narrow-minded like most of the men she had met. At the same time, he had valued her for what she was. He was one of the few men who had seen the courage inside her. Nemesis hoped she was right about him. She had never felt this much raw passion and desire for a man before. Perhaps she'd felt grateful in the past for men that had shown her respect, but it wasn't the same. John had understood a lot about her—had understood more than she had dared to hope.

Gareth led the way ahead of them. He walked with his head held high, while around twenty villagers trailed behind him, including a young mother cradling a baby. The road they would follow was rocky, and the ground cover of the Iron Mountain was thick with many trees scattered around. The light of the morning sun lit their path forward, while the chirping of birds filled the air. Nemesis stroked Alastor's coat and she felt the warmth of his body against her. Her steel breastplate hung from the saddle.

"I'm glad you're with us, Nemesis, even if you came here to kill Gareth."

Nemesis turned and saw Lady Alis, who was riding a small distance behind her on a grey horse. She wore clothes made of soft leather covered by a thin brown cloak. Nemesis had spoken to the lady a few times in the years she'd spent in Tyverdawn, although they had never become friends.

"I'm sorry about that," Nemesis said, ashamed.

"I know how difficult it is for a woman to obtain the respect of men and earn a place in Tyverdawn's Guard. I know how hard you've fought for it, and so I understand it couldn't be easy to leave everything behind."

Nemesis tugged on Alastor's reins, slowing down his gait to match Alis' pace. "My desire to prove my worth and earn respect blinded me. I had never considered that it was more important to have a place in the guard of a governor one respects. Walter has no honour."

"Most men in the north have no honour, Nemesis. My own father wanted to sell me like a broodmare to a rich lord, ignoring what I truly wanted. A land of morally corrupt men can hardly have a virtuous leader."

Nemesis frowned. "When I told my father that I wanted to become a warrior, he told me that if I hoped to have a good future, my best option was to become a nobleman's concubine." Nemesis said, feeling a familiar rage welling up inside her as she spoke. "Robert Thorn was a governor with honour."

"Truly," Alis agreed. "I hope that one day he will manage to punish his son for all he has done. Although, I must admit that I feel lucky for all that has happened. Walter's insurrection sent Gareth to my side. I never imagined I would find a man like him."

"You're lucky. I've never heard of a knight who would abandon his oaths for a woman before," Nemesis pointed out.

A sweet smile formed on Alis' rose-red lips. "He always tells me that he'll love me until his eyes can no longer behold the light of the moon," she said, casting a look at Gareth.

Nemesis remembered those words. Many in Tyverdawn had learned about that phrase and ridiculed Gareth, but she found it remarkable. Perhaps, in some distant land, there could be more men like him.

"I never expected that you would choose a man like John," Alis said after a bit.

"Me neither," Nemesis admitted with a laugh. "Though, I think he is—"

"Different," Alis said, finishing Nemesis' sentence for her. "I agree. Bounty hunters don't tend to go to secluded villages and remote mountains to live with a woman. At least, not any that I've met. I've seen the way he looks at you... He likes you more than you think."

Her words filled Nemesis with particular joy, and she stole a fleeting glance at John, who was riding idly some metres ahead. They continued their journey for what seemed like an hour, until she saw a few wooden houses on a little slope where the trees thinned out.

"We're here," Alis announced as Gareth and the villagers stopped within the smattering of houses.

Nemesis dismounted from Alastor and approached the wooden huts, gently tugging him along. Alis rode ahead to join Gareth and John pulled his horse to a stop.

"I like this place," John said, getting off his horse and approaching Nemesis.

Nemesis found the hillside peaceful and serene. Gareth came over to them with Alis. "That house on the left, the one with the large windows, is for you. There is a stable next to it," said the knight, looking at her and John.

Nemesis smiled with gratitude and they headed towards it with their horses. When she and John reached the stable, they tied up their steeds. Nemesis stroked Alastor one last time before heading to the entrance of the house Gareth had gestured towards.

John pushed the wooden door and they walked inside. The layout of the house was small with a few counters, a bed, and a modest hearth next to a window.

"I like it," John whispered in Nemesis' ear, and joy welled inside her once more.

Unexpected News

John walked between the trees, picking herbs. It had already been four days since they had first reached the hillside of the Iron Mountain, and everything had gone better than he hoped. By now, he had learned to pick the colour of the ahronth herb apart from the other native plants. John would have preferred Nemesis to come with him, but she was busy practicing with Gareth that morning. John had idly watched their training a few times, and he was convinced Nemesis was more capable with a sword than he was.

He continued looking for ahronth while thoughts circled around in his head. When they reached the Iron Mountain, he had been afraid he would be bored in a place like this. However, he had found that he enjoyed the life there. In the mornings he looked for herbs, while in the evenings he drank wine and rested in Nemesis' embrace. John had never imagined there could be a life like this for him.

A strange sound drew his attention—a sound that resembled wind rustling fallen leaves. John looked and felt that something was wrong. He had spent many years in remote places hunting runaways and wanted men and this sound reminded him of footfalls on leaves. He hid behind a tree and listened, but the sound had stopped. He waited for a little while in the quiet and decided he'd been wrong.

He hoisted himself up and stepped forward. Nobody was there. John looked at the sky. The sun's rays peeked through the thick leaves of the tall trees, dappling the ground with soft light. John kept on walking, increasing his speed. He needed to find a little more ahronth before he returned. Time had passed before he heard a loud neigh.

John hid once more behind the trunk of a tree, and two horses flashed past him. "Edric? Alan?" John called. He could swear his eyes were deceiving him.

The men heard his voice and turned around on their horses. The beasts were drenched in sweat, nostrils flaring and sides heaving.

"John! You need to leave here immediately!" Alan shouted. He looked terrified.

"What do you mean?" he asked and stepped into the open.

"We went back to Three Heads two days ago to find Walter's men there, along with someone else."

"Who?"

"Beric—The Golden Hand."

John's blood turned icy with the stark realization. "He turned us in?"

Alan nodded, sweat running down his face. "I heard that the bastard got wind of Gareth's true identity. He figured it out after seeing that men from the north were looking for him, pretending to be merchants. Beric found Gareth at his home and told him everything. He wanted to test the waters and see if he would be interested in hearing who was after him, hoping to trade gold for information. Then, in Gareth's house, he saw his cloak with the emblem of the knights of Gaeldeath, and recognised the symbols embroidered onto it. Beric assumed we were mercenaries that were sent to kill the knight and headed for Three Heads. He wanted to uncover who was hunting down Gareth."

Alan stopped to catch his breath.

"We also heard that he sent a few men to discreetly follow us and he found out we didn't kill Gareth, and that you had travelled to the Iron Mountain. We heard this two days ago. Beric sold this information to Walter's men for gold. Five of Gaeldeath's soldiers, along with one hundred mercenaries, are heading here for the purpose of killing you all. Walter's offering a huge bounty for Gareth's head," he finished, panting.

John was left speechless. He felt like time had stopped. He should have expected something like this might happen. It'd been too good to be true. Fate would cut his unexpected happiness short. He needed to run back, grab Nemesis and leave as soon as they could.

"Take me on your horse," John said.

Alan shifted forward in his saddle, and John mounted the horse to sit behind him. The steed started galloping quickly, side by side with Edric's horse. The giant man seemed unsettled. The trees were starting to thin out before them, and a few wooden houses appeared in the distance.

"Here, turn right!" John shouted.

Alan turned on his horse and they raced towards the houses. John saw Nemesis' chestnut hair waving in the wind. She was holding a sword while opposite her Gareth was demonstrating a complicated movement.

"Nemesis, Gareth, they found us!" John shouted as Alan pulled on the reins to stop his horse.

The knight spotted John and Alan riding up and an expression of horror etched itself into his features. "Who found us? What are they doing here?"

"Listen to me!" John shouted, and started explaining everything Alan told him while men and women gathered around them.

Gareth's eyebrows rose in fear, wrinkling his forehead. "We need to leave immediately," he said when John had finished speaking.

John hopped off his saddle and ran to Nemesis. Her gaze was both scared and sad. He could sympathise with her anguish. The men that were coming to the Iron Mountain had robbed them of their contentment.

Suddenly, a hunter's horn tore through the air with a deafening howl, and John knew it was too late. Alan and Edric weren't the only ones that had exhausted their horses to reach the Iron Mountain.

━━━━◆◆◆◆━━━━

Nemesis raised her sword in front of her face as dozens of horses started appearing before them. She saw Yorik, Gaeldeath's captain, looking down from his black horse with rage colouring his face. A hundred men approached them, enough to crush the two dozen men and women in their settlement.

"Good evening, Yorik," Gareth's voice rang out.

"I knew that I'd find you, bastard. Your time has come to pay." The rays of the sun passing through the sparse clouds made Yorik's armour glisten.

"If you want my head, come and take it. You don't need a hundred men to fight me."

Yorik's face reddened. "Soon, your head will decorate a spike in Tyverdawn."

"Don't be a coward, Yorik. You're a captain of Gaeldeath. Take me on yourself and take my head like a man with honour," Gareth insisted.

Around Yorik, Nemesis counted four more men that bore the red cloaks of Gaeldeath who she didn't recognise. The rest of the men that had set out to kill them were on horses, and they were clearly all mercenaries. It was hopeless.

"I know what you're trying to achieve, you imbecile. You won't get it. I won't fight you alone," Yorik shouted.

"Coward!" Gareth spat. "So, if you're faced with a knight in battle, you'll make a run for it? I'm sure that Walter wouldn't be too pleased to hear that." his tone dripped with disdain.

"Enough! Listen to me and shut your mouth, or I'll take Alis' head."

Nemesis was sure Yorik was prepared to go through with his threat as she watched Gareth turn red. She wondered why the Knight of The Moon was trying to provoke the captain under such dire circumstances. Perhaps, he hoped to goad Yorik into single combat, though that would hardly send the mercenaries away. She gripped her sword as Yorik's horse trotted towards them.

"Walter has a message for you," Yorik said. "You have two choices. I can either take your head and kill everyone in my way, or you'll come with me back to Tyverdawn and be pardoned under one condition."

Gareth's expression was unmoved. "What condition?"

"Every man with me today will lie with your lady. When we're done, we'll take you with us, while Alis and everyone on this land will be left to live. Nemesis will follow us to the north, where we will find a new way for her to atone for her crime. If she chooses to defy us again, she will be hanged."

Nemesis spotted Alis standing a few metres away, her face white as a sheet.

Nemesis raised her sword before Gareth had a chance to raise his own. "You're filthy scum—a bastard that will soon meet death, Yorik," she said.

"I'd choose my next words carefully, Nemesis. You're a woman who's betrayed her oath. Walter wants your head. However, if Gareth agrees to these terms, you can stay alive, while our governor will pick out a new punishment for you once we're back in Tyverdawn."

"You serve a man without honour... One day, you will die like a dog for what you've done!" Gareth snarled.

Yorik smiled sardonically. "Walter ordered me to give you a day to mull it over. We will set camp around the fringes of the mountain. If you try running away, we will slaughter you all. If I don't get the answer I want in the morning, we will kill every man, woman, and child in the area. Think about it carefully, Gareth."

Yorik's smile remained unfaltering. His eyes turned to John.

"I still wonder why you're the most famous bounty hunter," Yorik muttered, his expression filled with repulsion, before he turned and the other soldiers left.

"On your way here you passed by a village—did its people let you pass?" Gareth called out.

"At first, no. Though, when we killed one or two of them, they changed their minds." Yorik hadn't even cared to turn around as he threw the words over his shoulder.

The Hyenas of Fire

Terror and rage churned inside of Nemesis. She turned to Gareth who remained frozen, with his sword hanging limply from his right hand.

"What will we do?" Nemesis asked.

Gareth didn't speak while Alis approached them, lips and hands trembling.

"Why does Walter hate me so much? Why does everybody, even my own parents, hate me?" Alis asked, almost in a whisper.

Gareth turned to her and Nemesis saw a tear rolling down his cheek. "Walter doesn't care about you. The only thing he wants is to punish me for disgracing his name by leaving. More than that, he wants to torture me before I die. To make me choose between the death of innocents and the rape of the woman I love. Then, after he torments me, he will kill me."

Nemesis frowned. "If we return to Tyverdawn, he will have us both killed. If Yorik allows us to keep our heads, it will only be so Walter can take them with the whole of Gaeldeath watching. He will be thrilled to make an example of traitors," she said.

"We can't fight all those men. We only have two dozen people, and half of them are women that have never held a weapon. Even if the villagers from the fringes of the mountain help us, we'll all die."

"There are still two more villages near Long River. If everybody helps, perhaps there is a hope," Alis offered in an attempt to spark optimism.

"No." John's voice rang out.

Nemesis turned towards John.

"Our enemies not only know how to fight, but they have horses at their disposal. We don't have horses or archers. Even if a hundred villagers come to our aid with axes, they will be butchered. Most bounty hunters know their way around a sword and bow."

"John is right. Our only hope is to flee... Though, if we do that, they will slaughter every villager in the area," said Gareth.

The rest of the villagers had approached them, and Nemesis could see the terror in their faces. A young mother's arms trembled as she held her child.

"No. These people took me in. They accepted me as one of their own. I won't let them die for me! There are women, elderly, and children in these villages!" Alis shouted.

"We won't let these men rape you!" Nemesis would die to stop it. She admired the lady's honour and bravery. She could see herself in Alis and she would protect her no matter the cost.

"I'd rather die than allow something like that to happen!" Gareth said firmly.

"Perhaps there is another way," John said.

"There is no other way. You might be a good bounty hunter, but you don't know about battle. This is a battle that can't be won," the knight told him.

John grinned at Gareth's words. "That's a fact. Though, if those men set up camp along the road that leads here, near the fringes of the mountain, they'll find themselves among countless trees."

"So?" Gareth asked.

"We'll burn them. We'll kill everyone standing guard and set fire to the trees around them."

"The fire will spread here and kill us all," said Alis.

"No, there's enough distance between the houses and the forest, and if we head up the mountain, the fire will leave us unharmed. The smoke will be suffocating, but we will manage," John insisted.

"Perhaps the fire will spread towards the village! The villagers near the mountain's fringes will burn!" Alis insisted.

"There aren't any trees within two miles of the village. The villagers should be safe," Gareth said.

"That could work. I can help with the guards. I'm good with a bow," Alan spoke up.

Gareth brought his hand to his chin and glanced at Nemesis.

She returned his gaze with determination. "I think John's plan is our only hope," she said.

"If we fail, we're all doomed," Alis spoke.

"There is no other way. I won't let those men touch you," Gareth insisted.

John spoke up once more. "We will wait for nightfall, and then we'll inspect their encampments. Edric, Alan, and I will take care of the guards."

Longing swelled in Nemesis' chest. Something inside her was sure they'd make it. John's plan was the only thing that could save them.

"If we succeed, Walter might retaliate and send an army here. He will kill every soul he finds, even if we flee," Alis said.

"I don't think so. Walter wants Nemesis and me. If he learns that we're not here, he won't waste skilled soldiers to find us. Sure, he'll be seething, but he has too much on his plate to be wasting time on villagers."

"That man is a cowardly worm. He'll send a hundred mercenaries to kill one knight, but he couldn't face you in person," said Alan, looking at Gareth.

"Walter is the most dangerous man ever born. I've seen him kill five swordsmen in one stroke. I'm glad he isn't here," Gareth told him.

Nemesis understood Gareth's words all too well; she had witnessed Walter's prowess with her own eyes.

"Rest," the knight ordered. "We've got a long night ahead of us."

Men and women started heading off, and John cast a brief glance towards Nemesis as she walked behind him.

———◆○◆———

John had never put his faith in the gods, but in that moment, he wished that if they were indeed real, they would heed his prayers. He hoped they would make it out alive from what was to come. If they did, he and Nemesis would set off and head as far away as possible. They'd even reach the Western Empire if need be.

He looked around as he sat on a boulder near the wooden houses of the hillside. Countless times he'd warned Nemesis that Gareth's plan to live by the Iron Mountain was foolhardy. If the knight wanted to save Alis and the locals, he should have gotten as far away as possible. After all, if John could have tracked Gareth down, so could someone else. Amidst so many poor villagers, someone would be tempted to betray them for a little gold. John had tried to explain all this to Nemesis, but she seemed to put her whole trust in Gareth. She had even convinced John that nobody would even think to search the Iron Mountain, and that the villagers were loyal.

John let out a weary sigh. Perhaps that plan could have worked, had the Golden Hand not betrayed them. Perhaps the villagers could have kept their mouths shut. *Damn it*, John cursed the very moment he spoke to Beric. Had he never done so, chances are they wouldn't have been found.

"It's time to go," said Alan.

John turned and saw him by Edric's side. Night had fallen now, and they needed to start the fire as quietly as possible. They headed for the stable, mounted their horses, and rode like shadows in the darkness. Sweat dripped down his brow. He had never felt this kind of dread before. He constantly looked around him. Gareth had trusted them to execute this plan while the knight himself had stayed to defend the villagers.

They rode a little further until a sound that resembled hiccups reached John's ears. He gestured to Alan and Edric to be quiet, and they hopped off their horses carefully. They slowly headed to their right and tied the beasts to some nearby trees. The forest was thick in that area, providing good cover. John crouched down and took a few steps until he could make out a shape in the meagre light. A man was looking around aimlessly, bringing a flask to his lips. John grinned—bounty hunters were gormless drunkards. Nobody should trust them to keep watch since they couldn't act like real soldiers.

A sound like the rustling of leaves made John's hair stand on end as Alan's arrow buried itself into the man's head. The bounty hunter dropped to the ground, his flask rolling away from his limp hand.

"They chose the worst place to set up camp. Exactly where I thought they would," John whispered, recognising their surroundings. "Make a round and kill anyone you find. We'll wait for you here," he told Alan.

Alan nodded and skulked away into the darkness. Alan was one of the best archers John had ever met, and he knew better than anyone how to eliminate a target discreetly.

Time went by at a torturous pace while the only sound breaking the silence was Edric's breath. After a little while, John heard steps returning, and he raised his sword while his pulse hammered against his chest. He was ready to attack before he could make out a breathless Alan in front of him.

"They only had three guards keeping watch. They didn't expect we'd attack... I had a look at their camp and they all seemed to be asleep," he told John.

Of course. John had been sure they would be underestimated. He got up in one swift movement.

"Guard the horses," John ordered Edric.

John set off with Alan following behind him. He crouched as he walked, and briefly, his fingers brushed against the torch that was tied to his belt. They set off along a circular path, wanting to reach the road that led to the village in the mountain's fringes behind the sleeping soldiers. As time went on, he could tell apart some figures that were lying along the frozen moss of the ground. A shiver ran down his spine, and his palms were getting clammier by the moment until they reached their destination.

"You know what to do," he said, looking at Alan.

Alan unclasped a torch from his belt and a piece of flint. John did the same and rested the torch against the ground as he tried to start a fire with a small dagger. Sparks flew against the flint and gradually flames enveloped his torch. He held it up high and saw Alan holding his own flaming torch.

"Let's go," said John, and they ran off in opposite directions. They had agreed to set fire around their enemies.

John sprinted with all his strength, setting fire to tree branches in his wake. The wind was strong, making the fire grow and spread quickly. He kept on running, hoping for success. His legs hurt more by the moment. He started finding it harder to catch his breath as flames licked and spread to the trees a few metres away from him. Soon, he'd meet back up with Alan.

Just a little further, he told himself, trying to regain courage before he saw the figure of a man running towards him.

"Our horses," said John as soon as Alan was facing him.

They threw their torches to the ground and started running towards Edric's direction until they found him with the reins in hand.

"We have to go. Now!" John barked.

The three of them jumped on their horses and rode like lightning, the wind tearing at them while the forest burned behind.

⸺⬦⸺

John dismounted from his mare as he pulled the horse to a stop in front of Nemesis and Gareth. Flames lit up the night sky in the distance.

"We did it," he said, and they smiled with relief. "They'll burn, all of them."

"Your plan was genius," Gareth admitted.

John grinned until he felt something cold hit his forehead. His stomach churned as he looked up at the sky, his heartbeat quickening within his chest.

Raindrops started pouring down with force, and John looked into Nemesis' dark eyes, her expression stunned. John was sure that if the gods were real, they weren't intending to grant them any peace.

The Moon and the Tiger

"Maybe the fire managed to burn them first," Nemesis offered.

It didn't take long before the rain stopped, and the glow of the flames had faded from the sky.

"We'll wait a little longer," said Gareth from behind the trunk of a tree.

Nemesis outstretched her hand to touch John's. He smiled at her under the soft moonlight, but she understood—that smile wasn't real. John was terrified. They had decided to hide behind a few trees west of the wooden houses. Nobody had taken a horse, as it would be harder to stay hidden. If any of their enemies were still alive, they could attack at any point, and they wanted to keep the element of surprise on their side.

Nemesis was the only one who wore her steel breastplate, though her arms and legs weren't armoured. She glanced at Gareth a few metres away. The knight's clothes were solely wool since he hadn't travelled with his armour to the villages of Oldlands.

Hidden between the trees, there were only fourteen people—the ones who could handle a sword—while the women had fled further up the mountain. Gareth had advised them to go as far as they could climb, though Nemesis knew they wouldn't get too far in the deep darkness of the night.

Heavy footfalls reached her ears, and her heart squeezed as she tried to make out where the sound was coming from.

"Burn it all down!" a voice shouted.

A sharp tug pulled at Nemesis' hand, and she saw John's frozen stare. Just metres away from them, a few dozen men on horses appeared between the trees. Some held their swords while others carried large torches.

"Find Alis. That high-born slut is going to pay. I'll make sure Gareth watches as we fuck her."

Nemesis recognised Yorik's voice. She tried to get a better look. She was willing to bet that more than fifty men had survived the fire. A strange sound reached her ears, and John's hand jerked once more in hers. Nemesis watched with horror as a body hit the ground. The fletching of an arrow stuck out of Eric's skull—one of the peasants—a few metres away from her.

"There they are! Between the trees!" someone called out.

Gareth drew his sword and ran towards the nearest horse to slice off its front legs. The beast screamed, and Gareth pierced through its rider's head with one sharp thrust. Nemesis ran forward too, letting out a wild battle cry. John, Alan, Edric, and the villagers followed her lead.

Nemesis ran between the trees and noticed a man aiming at her with a bow. She twisted sharply but an arrow buried itself in the skull of her enemy. Looking to her right, she saw Alan with his bow raised. A sword swung for her head, and she blocked it with her blade, then stabbed the rider through the thigh. The man screamed in agony, and his mare reared up. Nemesis sliced off the back leg of the horse, and then a second arrow grazed by her head. Another archer aimed for her from his steed and she lunged for him.

Nemesis tried to injure his leg once she was in front of him. He tugged on his reins, and his horse turned sharply and threw her to the ground. She saw the rider raising his bow toward her head when a black horse threw itself violently against her enemy. Nemesis saw a peasant on Alastor's back.

"Get on!" he yelled at her.

Nemesis scrambled to her feet and went to mount Alastor, just as an arrow pierced through her horse's skull.

"No!"

The horse crumbled to the ground and Nemesis kneeled next to it with tears in her eyes. She saw the villager trying to drag his crushed leg from under the animal's body, before an arrow embedded itself in his eye. Nemesis stood as ten men surrounded her with arrows nocked in their bows.

"Throw your sword aside!" one of them demanded.

Nemesis wanted to kill them all. She knew she stood a chance if only she could take them on one by one, but she wouldn't be given that chance.

"Throw your sword aside, woman! Otherwise, I'll pluck your eyes out and fuck you like a whore."

Nemesis threw her sword with all her might and it buried itself into the head of the man who spoke. An arrow hit her bicep and she collapsed to the ground. The pain coursed like fire through her arm. Arms hoisted her up and dragged her roughly. She was blinded with pain though she tried to force her eyes open. There wasn't much light around her. The men dragged her between the trees, and she saw the villagers that had fought by her side, now dead and full of arrows. Tears spilled down her cheeks. A gigantic man was lying face down with a sword stabbed through him—Edric was dead, too.

She looked for John, but couldn't find him anywhere—or Gareth. They kept dragging her until she could make out the wooden houses by the side of the mountain—the houses where she had hoped to spend peaceful moments by John's side. Five men in red cloaks were gathered beside a kneeling figure.

Nemesis tried to push her captors away. They glared at her menacingly. "I can walk by myself just fine."

The men ignored her and kept on dragging her toward the soldiers. Nemesis saw Yorik's face in the dim light. In front of him, Gareth was collapsed on his knees, an arrow shot through his elbow.

"Excellent," said Yorik, looking towards her. "This one we won't kill. We'll make her a whore when we return to Tyverdawn."

Nemesis looked him in the eyes, and with a wolfish grin, spat in his face.

———◆○◆———

John's blood ran cold. He could hear their words from where he remained hidden behind a tree. He and Alan had killed three men on their horses but had soon retreated between the trees when arrows started raining down on them. They were hiding in the hollow trunk of a tree next to the wooden houses.

"What can we do?" he whispered.

"Nothing," Alan said flatly. "They're dead. I'm sorry, John."

John peered out and saw Nemesis next to Gareth. He knew that whatever awaited both her and the knight would be terrifying.

"Where is that highborn slut? Where is Alis?" Yorik demanded.

"You'll never find her," Gareth replied.

John admired the knight's valour, and Nemesis' too. He saw Nemesis spit in Yorik's face before he planted his fist in her nose. He thought about doing something but he couldn't find the courage.

Yorik laughed. "I'm sure that she ran up the mountain with the rest of the women. They won't get away," he said.

John could see and hear everything. He felt a hand tug gently at his shoulder, and he turned around to see Alan.

"They'll see you," the man warned him.

"I don't care anymore," John replied. He had decided to do something. He had to try to find a way to help Nemesis and Gareth.

"Just take my head and go back to your lord, Yorik." Gareth's voice rung out.

John turned once more to watch the Knight of The Moon.

Yorik laughed again. "You don't get it, Gareth... Alis won't make it out of here, and you'll watch as we ravage her, again and again. I won't kill you—I want you to see everything. After we're done, I'll take her head, and burn you; I'll burn you just as you tried burning us."

The fear on Gareth's face was palpable. "You're scum! You're a man without honour!" Gareth's self-control had evaporated, and tears started to roll down his flushed face.

"Find the women!" Yorik ordered. "You'll see, Gareth... You really thought you could win—thought you stood a chance against one of Walter Thorn's men. The white tiger of the House of Thorn will swallow the half-moon of your house once and for all."

Everything happened almost instantly. Nemesis threw something towards Gareth, and he caught it in mid-air. John saw the Knight of the Moon look at the dagger with grateful eyes.

Yorik yelled as Gareth turned the dagger to his chest and stabbed it into his heart. John wanted to scream, but a sword cut through Nemesis' throat.

Nemesis was trying to breathe, blood bubbling out of her throat, until she lay still on the ground. *No, no!* Tears poured out of John's eyes. The only woman he had ever loved had been killed before his eyes, and he could only watch helplessly. He drew the thin sword at his belt and poised himself to attack—to charge towards death—when he heard Yorik's voice.

"You fool! Why did you kill her?" the captain yelled to the Gaeldean soldier.

"I thought she'd attack us! I got worried when she tossed the dagger."

Hatred filled John's soul—pure hate. Once more, he poised himself to run and spear Yorik through the skull with all his might. He didn't care about dying, so long as the captain followed him in death. He couldn't kill Walter, but Yorik's life was the best he could hope for. He took a deep breath and went to run when an arrow pierced through Yorik's head.

John froze and pulled himself back into the treetrunk. Alan had sprung out from where he stood and shot Yorik.

Before John could move, Alan's body staggered back as a dozen arrows struck him. It was all over. Opposite him, John could see the door of one of the wooden houses. Now that Yorik had died, John had to live. If he managed to do that, he could take revenge on Walter.

Jumping to his feet, he ran for the door and pushed it open. Smoke hung in the room as he made for an open window and dove outside. John sprinted along the perimeter of the house into another thicket of trees. Looking hesitantly behind him, he didn't see anyone following him. The trees obstructed his vision. He took a few more steps, and he saw Gaeldean soldiers in the distance.

"There's no one else. He was the only one that made it out," a tall Gaeldean soldier said.

"Damn it! Yorik is dead!" another called out. "Let's go find the women."

"Where is John, the Long Arm? I didn't see his corpse anywhere," said another man.

An invisible hand squeezed John's heart.

"Who cares about him? We're here for them," the taller Gaeldean soldier said and gestured towards Nemesis' and Gareth's corpses. "Unfortunately, they died sooner than we'd have liked... Let's hope we find the women so they can make it up to us for all that happened."

John's stomach churned as he looked at Nemesis' lifeless form. Her dark eyes that had been once full of life stared sightlessly at the sky. He was a coward. He had wanted to save her, but he was weak. John saw the men mounting their horses and passing by the houses, heading up into the mountain. He started running. If he wanted to live to take revenge, he needed to run as far as possible. He stopped after a few moments. He knew he had to flee, but needed to make sure Alis was safe. Now that Yorik was dead, perhaps the rest of the soldiers would decide to leave if they couldn't find Alis quickly enough.

John ran after them, keeping his distance. Nemesis' black eyes—the gaze he adored—wouldn't leave his mind. He wished with all his heart that Alis would make it. Something inside him told him that would be a redemption; that Nemesis' soul would find peace in the kingdoms of the dead if Alis didn't die today.

"There they are!"

John's heart stopped once more as a voice shouted nearby. He changed direction and headed right. The bodies of horses littered the ground in front of him while around fifty enemies stood ready.

"Time to exact part of our payment," said one of the soldiers.

John took a few more steps, trying to get a clearer view without being noticed.

"I'm sure they'll enjoy it," another voice added.

John tried to approach silently, and he finally saw what the rest of the men did. A dozen women stood in line, holding each other's hands, while at the very end there was the young woman with her baby in her arms. Lady Alis stood at the centre of the line. They had nowhere to run, standing at the edge of a cliff.

"You won't take anything from us," said Alis.

"We'll take everything! Your bodies and your lives!" a man called out with glee.

"The only thing you will receive is the fury of the gods!" Alis replied.

John would have sworn that time stopped. In horror, he watched as the lady smiled, and with one sharp turn, faced the cliff. The rest of the women followed her, and all at once, they leaped into the void.

The Payment

John watched Tom—the first villager he had met in his trip to find Gareth—as he threw a pouch of gold into the merchant's hands.

"I sold you my best wares," the merchant said, laughing.

Tom laughed as well. "I know. You truly are the best merchant that passes by these parts." The fading light of the evening sun lit Tom's plain brown clothes and the green silk vest of the merchant.

The man tied the pouch to his belt, his smile unfaltering.

John started walking slowly into the village without taking his eyes off the two men. His right hand gripped the hilt of his sword and drew it with force.

"Give me your hands," John said, pointing his sword at the man.

The merchant turned towards John and his eyes widened. He prepared to run, but Tom grabbed him firmly and held him in place. The villagers had decided to punish this man for what he had done.

"But how? How are you alive?" the merchant asked.

"Your hands. Give me your hands," said John, voice shaking with rage.

Beric, the Golden Hand, outstretched his hands at the height of his chest, trembling as horror filled his eyes.

"I did what you would, too. How many men have you killed for gold?" Beric stammered.

John smiled grimly. "I've paid for all I've done. Now, it's time for you to pay. These hands, the hands that accepted gold in return for my life, belong to me."

In one stroke, John brought down his sword and the man's hands hit the ground. Screaming filled the air and blood gushed out from where Beric's elbows once were.

"I'll take your arms with me. Perhaps they'll bring me the same good fortune they brought you," John shouted over the man's screaming.

Beric continued squealing, and Tom shoved him roughly to the ground.

"This is payment for all you did to the villagers that kept you in business all these years. You didn't only betray Gareth, but us, too," the man said and kicked his back. Tom turned to John. "Kill him."

"No... I'd rather let him live without his arms," John replied, wiping his blade off on his trousers.

"There aren't any healers here. He won't live too long."

"I meant for the little time he has left."

Tom nodded and started walking away, and John followed him.

"Help! Help!" Beric squealed, looking at the peasants that worked ahead of him.

"Nobody will help you, Golden Hand," John replied, and continued walking away as he returned his sword to its scabbard.

⊕

John brought his flask to his mouth and swigged a mouthful of wine watching the moon. Three days had passed since Nemesis had died, though it felt like an eternity. The woman he'd loved was dead, and his companions had followed her. Gareth and Alis had taken their own lives—everybody had died. John had sworn to himself he wouldn't leave this land until Beric was dead, and with the villagers' help, he'd managed it.

The events of the past days plagued his mind endlessly. The bounty hunters and Walter's men had decided to leave the Iron Mountain when the women had thrown themselves off the cliffside. John had seen them march down. He'd followed them cautiously on a mare he'd found near the wooden houses—the place where he'd spent the best days of his life. By the time the soldiers had reached the base of the mountain, they were met with a hundred villagers wielding axes. Walter's men had killed three peasants on their way to Gareth, and the news had spread to every village in the area. The villagers had sought to defend their land, and the bounty hunters had agreed to leave without any bloodshed. The fire had killed half of them, and they didn't want to risk another battle.

John felt an emptiness inside him. He was sure he would feel redemption when Beric died, but watching the man dying hadn't changed anything inside him. The villagers had decided to help him once they found out that Beric was the man behind everything that had happened, the man who had sent countless people to their death.

"What will you do?" a voice asked.

John looked at the man, Tom. He wished he could turn back time and do everything differently, but unfortunately, that wasn't possible.

"I'll go to Iovbridge," said John after a bit.

"To the royal capital? Why?" Tom asked.

"War is coming. Walter is crueller than I thought. Soon, he and the king will throw themselves into battle and the kingdom will be rife with death."

"Then leave Knightdorn. Do you want to fight for the king?"

"I don't know. All I know is that the north is no longer safe."

They stayed silent for a few moments.

"Have a safe journey, Long Arm," said Tom after a moment.

John stood up and shook the man's hand before heading for his mare. Thoughts swirled through his mind. Something inside him called for him to join the king's side in Iovbridge—to take revenge on Walter for Nemesis. However, the voice of reason told him he wasn't a warrior.

He sighed, exhausted. He couldn't decide what to do. Still, perhaps in Iovbridge he'd find the answer. He could either fight or stay there, far from the north, at least until Walter was defeated. Besides, if the royal capital didn't suit him, he could leave whenever he wished.

John approached his steed and loosened its reins from a rock. He cast one last look towards the village and jumped onto the horse. Flicking its reins, he rode like the wind, disappearing into the darkness.

About the Author

Gregory Kontaxis was born in Athens. He studied Informatics and Finance in Greece and the United Kingdom, and he has worked as a Financial Analyst in Vienna and London. He currently resides in London, where he busies himself with investment risk management and writing. *The Return of the Knights* is the first book of his pentalogy, *The Dance of Light*.

From Gregory Kontaxis

If you enjoyed this story, please consider leaving a review on Amazon. It would mean so much to me. And if you are on Goodreads, would you share your thoughts with friends and followers?

You can also find all of my latest writing news by subscribing to my website at https://www.gregorykontaxis.com

By Gregory Kontaxis

The Dance of Light

Book 1: The Return of the Knights